HERITAGE IN POWDERSMOKE

Nels Ondane, breaking his back working from dawn to dusk for his uncle, a rigorous employer, dreamed of going West to claim some free land; but his uncle objected to traveling to what he considered heathen country. The news was received that the uncle's only brother had died, leaving everything to the two surviving Ondanes as the next of kin. But to inherit they had to go to the dead man's last resting place, wherever that might be, to erect some sort of marker above his grave. It seemed a reasonable if slightly unusual request and, startlingly, the estate amounted to a considerable sum: ten thousand dollars. So the older man's objections to leaving civilization were overcome and, with his nephew, he set out for the violence and lawlessness of the last frontier . . .

HERITAGE IN POWDERSMOKE

CHAPTER ONE

A sudden shower had blown up out of the Alleghenies, threatening a deluge. Nels Ondane, who had been methodically packing sacks of potatoes from the outdoor root cellar to the wagons, hastened his stride. Only a couple of sacks remained, and he swept them both up, one under either arm, the two-hundred-pound burden scarcely slowing his pace.

The driver hastily adjusted a weathered tarp above the load and drove away, hunched against the storm. August Millard, who as usual had contrived to appear busy while allowing Nels to do most of the work, swiped a mixture of sweat and rain from his face with a shirt-sleeve and turned hastily toward the weather-beaten shack which they had called home for the last year.

'Thank goodness we're rid of those spuds,' he observed, a complaining note in his voice. 'Two bits a hundred! The one year in ten that we have a good crop, the price is so poor that they're hardly worth digging. Well, that does it. No more Pennsylvania for me. I figure we'll do better headin' back for York State again.'

Nels did not bother to reply. There was no profit in reminding his uncle that the price had been forty cents when they had dug the crop the previous fall, and that it was his stubbornness which had made him hold on while the price continued to drop.

His Aunt Mary straightened from the range, the pervading aromas of good food filling the room from the briefly opened oven door. No matter how little she had to work with, somehow she always managed a tasty meal. Her flushed face betrayed anxiety as she caught her husband's remark, but she too, forebore to comment. Looking at her, Nels felt a guilty twinge at his own resolve. It would be hard to leave her, tied so firmly to the endless treadmill of existence with a hopelessly impractical dreamer.

For that was what life with August Millard amounted to, a treadmill which led nowhere. For as long as Nels could remember, they had moved each year, always to a new but run-down farm, with fresh high hopes that by doing so things would somehow be better. The hope belonged mostly to August, who was incurably optimistic about what lay over the next hill, but whose enthusiasm faded swiftly in the face of the reality of hard work under a blazing summer sun.

A farmer had always to contest with the elements, so there was a certain logic in August's perpetual excuses for failure. One year it would be drought, grasshoppers another, hail a third and, when everything was favorable and the crop was bountiful, starvation prices for their produce. That poor management might be a contributory factor, August refused to concede.

Over the last decade, Nels had increasingly shouldered the work load, seeing his efforts go for nothing. Now he was tempted to point out his uncle's oft-repeated promise: that this time they would stay in one place, not moving again. The land here was good, and the crop had been bountiful. Aunt Mary had once wailed that she was weary unto death of the endless moving to a new place. If they stayed, a place might in time be made to seem like home.

August Millard was like the wild geese honking north through the night. With each successive spring he had to move on. Hitching his chair closer to the table, he talked on eagerly.

'I heard tell only yesterday of a place east in York State, down Deposit way. They say it's wonderful corn country. We'll get packed and going, find us a new farm in time to plant a crop—'

Neither noticing nor heeding the silence of his wife and nephew, he talked on. It was only as he scraped back his chair, replete, that he thought to ask their opinion. 'Don't it sound good to you two?'

Mary's reply was a mixture of resignation and despair.

'Since you want to go, I suppose we will.'

'I figure we've *got* to,' August pointed out earnestly. 'Once we find the right place, things are bound to be better. A man's a fool to waste his time where everything's against him. What we need, and will have, one of these days, is land of our own. Eh, Nels?'

'Perhaps.' Nels took the plunge. He had been dreading it, knowing the explosion which would follow, hating to leave his Aunt. Since he had been orphaned at the age of three, she had been like a mother. August, too, had been good, in his way. Still, if he owed August anything, he'd more than paid it back, doing a man's work these last dozen years.

'I'm going to head West,' he went on. 'Way West—Montana or thereabouts. There's free land out there, and I aim to have some of it.'

August regarded him as though he had spoken heresy. Intensely religious, August held strong convictions in regard to the country beyond the Mississippi. Not only was the land wild and lawless; it was heathenish. The West in itself would not have been so bad; it was Montana which he held in particular abhorrence. That was the country of his brother-in-law, Bart Ondane.

'Montana,' he repeated. 'That Godless country—'

Mary gave a little cry and jumped to her feet, clearly thankful for a chance at diversion. She darted to the what-not in a corner.

'Mercy me, I almost forgot. Mr. Wimpole stopped by while you men were working, and left a letter that the post office asked him to deliver. It's post marked from somewhere in Montana.'

Mail of any sort, and especially letters, were so rare that they made infrequent visits to the post office. Astonishment constrained August's tongue. He accepted the letter, staring at it, turning it over and over, as though it might be dangerous. It was long and impressive-looking. The postmark which Nels made out was unfamiliar. Mocking Bird.

His mind jumped to the obvious conclusion. The only person who might conceivably be writing to them from out there would be Uncle Bart, which in this household was a forbidden name. Bart Ondane was the black sheep of the family. He had gone west nearly a quarter of a century before, after which only vague but rather dreadful rumors had drifted back. Rarely had he written, and no letter had come for the last dozen years. It had been assumed that he must have come to a bad end.

Fourteen years ago he had returned for a visit, dropping in without warning. Nels still remembered the excited warmth in his aunt's face, his own pleasure. A big man, Bart Ondane had brought the breath of wide-open spaces, a hint of forbidden things. One day he had demonstrated his handiness with a Colt forty-five. Another time he had performed what to Nels' eyes was sheer magic with a rope.

That week had left its impress upon Nels. In the succeeding years, sometimes secretly, often painfully, he had taught himself to use a rope, a revolver, a bull whip; to ride as he fancied a cowboy would. Bart Ondane might be all that was whispered about him, but he had remained a hero to his nephew.

The visit had been cut short when the two men had quarreled. Bart had headed back West, into the silence. Mary never mentioned her scapegrace brother, but now her cheeks held a faint glow.

'Thomas J. Crockett, Attorney at Law.' August read the return address, frowning. 'Now what could this be?' He opened the envelope and drew out a letter, addressed to all three of them. Again he puzzled over that.

'Now why'd this be addressed to you, Nels, as well as to your Aunt Mary and myself? Must have something to do with Bart. No doubt his sins have caught up with him at last, and I presume that you two are his only surviving kin—not that there's anything of which to be proud. If this lawyer wants money to defray his funeral expenses, I'm afraid he's out of luck.'

His surmise was at least partly correct. The

letter conveyed the news that Bart Ondane was indeed dead, and since his sister and nephew were his only living relatives, the lawyer was getting in touch with them.

The next paragraph was a surprise. The black sheep had turned out to be not quite the ne'er-do-well which they had always supposed. He had left property—an inheritance to be shared jointly by sister, brother-in-law and nephew. Its total worth was in the neighborhood of ten thousand dollars.

'Ten thousand dollars!' August repeated, and looked up, considerably shaken. 'I can hardly believe it! To think that such a worthless—'

He clamped his lips on the word, amending it carefully. 'From all that I knew of Bartholomew, I am surprised. And now he is dead. Poor Bart. Your only surviving brother, Mary. And my brother-in-law, of course. I suppose I should grieve, but after all these years, that would be difficult.' His voice quickened.

'But ten thousand dollars, left to us! Mary, this is a dream come true! Why, it's the hand of fate!'

Mary nodded wordlessly. After a quarter of a century moving from one rented farm to another, each a little poorer than the preceding one, she had learned to live with disillusion. News of wealth, coming at this particular time, seemed too good to be true. As it would probably turn out to be, she reflected, once all the details were known.

August talked on, with quickening excitement. Tall, black-bearded, he had the look of a patriarch, the eyes of a visionary. All his life had been spent in dreaming, making new moves in pursuit of a will-o'-the-wisp, pursuing impossible plans.

'I've wanted something like this all my life,' he exclaimed. 'Land! Land of our own, the good earth, a spot where we can be masters of our own destiny! Land—and most of all, a ranch. That must be what this is, for the West is a land of ranches. I was beginning to fear that I cherished an impossible dream, one which could never come true. Now, all at once—thanks to Bart, and may the Good Lord forgive me such unkind thoughts as I may have had concerning him!—now, when we need it most, this comes to pass!'

He drew a sighing breath, half-turning to Nels.

'You never saw your Uncle Bart but the one time, did you, Nels? You were just a little shaver at the time, but he took a great fancy to you. Too bad he couldn't have stayed longer. I urged him to. But he was a fiddle-footed man. Long afterward, we heard that he was in Montana, ranching, apparently. Now, according to what this letter says, he has passed on, leaving his ranch to me—to us. I never anticipated anything like this—having learned to expect nothing from anyone, save my own toil and sweat.'

'The letter says that Nels and I are his only living kin?' Mary asked. 'Then apparently he never married.'

No one referred to Bart's bitter declaration, made when he had run away from home, an assertion that he hated everyone and never wanted to see any of them again. Except for that one surprise visit, years later, he never had.

There was more in the letter, a clause in Bart's will, something so strangely sentimental that it seemed out of place. To inherit, they—or one of them—must proceed to Bart's last resting place, wherever that might be, there to erect some sort of a marker above his grave. Still, it seemed a reasonable enough request.

According to the lawyer, Bart Ondane had ridden away from Mocking Bird on business, a journey of several days duration. Then word had come back of his sudden illness in a small and distant town named Highcard, of his death among strangers, and a lonely grave.

Mary listened, stony-faced. August dabbed at his eyes with a blue bandana.

'He must have foreseen something of the sort—perhaps a premonition. Well, of course we'll attend to it, once we arrive in that country. We can scarcely do less, under the circumstances.' He became brisk. 'Fortunately, there's nothing to hold us here. We'll take the first possible train West.'

CHAPTER TWO

During the first day's ride westward, August Millard bubbled like a kettle of stew. Thereafter, as they rolled farther and farther in a land ever wider and less crowded, he grew unwontedly sober. Their destination was the country which he had always feared and hated.

Leaving the train after several days, they proceeded by stagecoach. Much of the time they were the only passengers, in a land ever wider, higher, more lonely. Houses were virtually nonexistent. The driver explained that they were usually set well back from the road, out of sight.

'People out here like to be sort of private, and not too crowded,' he explained with a wave of his whip. 'When you can look out and see another man's smoke, that's too close.'

Mocking Bird, in local parlance, had been shortened to Mockery. Not only was it the only town in that part of the country; it was half a hundred miles from the nearest neighboring village.

Fifty miles! Mary caught her breath, trying to keep the gasp inaudible. That was a long day's drive, with horses and buggy. It was also likely that it would be many additional miles from the town to the ranch.

Nels rode most of the time with the driver, eager, listening, saying little. Inside the stage, August was silent also. He could guess his wife's thoughts. This was frontier country, big with promise, but lonely. If anything should go wrong—

For the first time he had a feeling that perhaps he was letting her down, by coming out here, even more than in the past.

Furtively he watched her, where she sat on the opposite seat, struck anew by her good looks. Her hair was thick and lustrous, still dark brown, with only a faint sprinkling of silver. But where gaiety had lurked about the corners of lips and eyes, gravity had come instead. Were such changes the natural result of the years, or did they come from disappointments, from hope too often deferred?

Was he asking too much of her, to leave behind the life she had known? There had never been much time to make firm friends; still, it would take a lot to make up for such comforts as a doctor in an adjoining village, and neighbors within sight or even shouting distance. Not to mention the church, on a

Sunday morning—

He had been reared a religious man, and he clung stubbornly to his faith, deriving strength from it. Only there would probably be no church out here; the rising mountains would be the nearest thing to a cathedral.

Mary had always been loyal, ready and willing to go wherever he had thought best, doing her share and more. They had traipsed from one run-down farm to another, move following move as the years followed one another. And for what? He had talked big, but the net results of the years had added up to mighty small potatoes.

How many times had he promised her that with their next move, life was going to be different, better, easier for her, with a better house in which to live, luxuries instead of bare necessities, a home fit for a woman.

This time it must be, it should be different. The rising hills, the vastness of the land, made him strangely humble.

The hills hemmed them in now, rearing to either side, forming a gateway to a great valley. The driver's voice, explaining to Nels, came clearly.

'This is Powdersmoke Pass, the only good route into the Valley of the Gun. It's a big place, the Gun—more'n a dozen ranches in the valley and the mountains surrounding, and mostly they ain't crowded. There's another road of sorts from the southwest, off

Highcard way—but it ain't used much. Closed by snow a good part of the year, anyway.'

Powdersmoke Pass to the Valley of the Gun! Nels felt his pulse quicken. With such a pass the only gateway, it had probably come by its name naturally. The hills shut them in, causing darkness at noonday. At least the shadows were long.

The day was growing old when they sighted the town, sprawled athwart the lower limits of the pass. After the empty miles it was a relief. Most of the buildings, though rising impressively, were false-fronted. Hitch-rails held a few scattered horses, and a team was attached to a buckboard. Houses were scattered about as chance or fancy dictated, with little semblance of order. Most were in need of paint.

The Gun valley opened out to the south, rugged, breath-taking.

Only two buildings looked fresh and prosperous. The signs across the fronts of both indicated the reason. One read simply: 'Saloon;' the other 'Powdersmoke Saloon.'

August observed them with a jaundiced eye. He was liking what he saw less and less.

'I suppose those are the places that make money, here as in New York or Pennsylvania,' he observed bitterly. 'Bloodsuckers, preying on the weaknesses of their fellow-men!'

With him, the subject was a sore one. It had always been his contention that liquor had been the ruin of Bart Ondane, driving him from a proper civilization, and finally bringing him to an untimely death. Whiskey was a wrecker, rum a demon, evils to be shunned yet battled.

Several loungers awaited the arrival of the stage. One man came forward, looking out of place in a business suit. His hand-clasp was warm, but Nels observed that his eyes remained frostily watchful.

'I'm Tom Crockett,' he explained. 'Glad to see you folks. I sort of had a hunch that you might get in today, so I dropped around to meet the stage. I expect you're tired, so perhaps we'd better get across to your place, where you can have a chance to rest and freshen up. We can talk any time, tomorrow if you like.'

'To relax would be welcome,' August agreed, somewhat puzzled. He looked around uncertainly. 'But you speak as though the place were right at hand, sir?'

Crockett laughed a shade self-consciously. Nels took note that his vest was of red and white checks. He wore a ring with a huge yellowish stone, a gold nugget.

'Didn't I give details of your place in my letter?' he asked. 'I must have neglected to do so, but no harm done. It's right at hand, right across the street, in fact. Take a look at it.

Powdersmoke Saloon! You folks are the owners of the biggest and best saloon anywhere for a hundred miles around!'

CHAPTER THREE

Nels, alone of the three, was not too surprised. He had been remembering his Uncle Bart, recalling what little he'd known of him in that long-ago week. There had been a breath-taking quality about Bart, but in retrospect there seemed considerable justification for August's opinion of him. And the stage-driver, discovering that his name was Ondane, had eyed him queerly and changed the subject.

August was shocked. His face reddened, and he slowly set down the pair of carpetbags which he had been carrying.

'Saloon!' he repeated, and his glance went to the well-painted structure which Crockett designated. Unlike most of the other business houses, this was not false-fronted. The Powdersmoke Saloon had two stories, with an outside stairway leading to the second floor.

'Surely you're joking?' August protested. 'It was my understanding that my brother-in-law owned a ranch.'

'Why, so he does—I mean, he did,' Crockett agreed. 'But this is what he designated in his will as being your heritage. He told me that with this saloon and the business it did, you would be well provided for—very well indeed. As he remarked, folks always buy liquor, whether they can afford it or not. Those who like to drink will get the stuff, no matter what, good times or bad.'

'A saloon!' August repeated, still unbelieving. 'A gift from Bart! It's what we might have expected from him!'

'Yes,' the lawyer agreed. 'He remarked to me, while he was making this particular provision, that he knew just how much you'd appreciate a saloon!'

With the first shock over, anger was building in August, fed by old memories, which he had sought to suppress since learning of Bart's demise, coupled with what had seemed like generosity. Now he understood that the gesture, like most things done by Bart Ondane, had been both a sham and a mockery. Even in the making of his will, he had thought only of playing a joke on a brother-in-law, who he knew hated liquor above everything else, and to whom the word saloon spelled sin. He had set a trap, baiting it with avarice, to spring from beyond the grave.

August closed his eyes, lifting his face to the sky. He made a patriarchal figure. He reached out suddenly, closing the fingers of one hand on the lawyer's arm, in a grip which made Crockett cringe.

'You were mighty careful to say nothing about what this inheritance might consist of when writing us about it,' he growled. 'Not a word concerning a saloon, not even a hint. Am I right in supposing that Bart put you up to that?'

Crockett eyed him uneasily. He had understood enough to appreciate the hidden humor in the situation, but there was a difference between fulfilling a request and carrying the joke to unnecessary lengths.

'That is correct, sir. He gave me definite instructions as to how it should be done in the event of any contingency. Since I was acting as his attorney, of course I respected his wishes.'

Nels was listening with careful attention. From the things he'd heard of his uncle Bart, the festering hate he'd cherished for his kinfolk, such a joke seemed in keeping with the man. Even so, something was wrong, as though the carefully placed figures in a chess set had been jarred out of place.

The lawyer squirmed as the fingers bit deeper, then staggered as he was violently released.

'Mocking and unregenerate, even to the last,' August breathed, 'as were his words to me, when he came to visit us more than a decade ago, ostensibly in friendship. "I've found a way to get back at you," he told me at the time. "I've planted the seeds, and some have fallen upon fertile ground. Your son admires me; moreover, he's an Ondane! I'll make sure that he follows in *my* footsteps, not yours!" And he laughed as I told him to go, never to darken my door again!'

August was breathing heavily. Mary and Nels listened in amazement. Never before had he revealed the cause of that quarrel.

'Still, he is gone to his reward, and may the Lord have mercy on his soul,' August added more quietly. Looking up, the fire returned to his eyes. 'But what a twisted mind! This, then—this place of debauchery—is our inheritance, and only this?'

Crockett regarded him uneasily. A small crowd was gathering, listening while dusk closed down from the mountains which towered above the town.

'I'm afraid that's the size of it, Mr. Millard. This was his bequest to the three of you. Of course, if you are opposed to such a business, you can easily dispose of it. The Powdersmoke Saloon is a profitable enterprise, and will find a ready sale—'

'A profitable enterprise, you say, sir, to sell liquor to men enslaved in the toils of so hellish a habit, for the debauchery of soul and body!' August roared. 'No doubt it's a money-maker, since many engage in it! But do you think for one moment that I would profit from blood money, sir, that I would be a party to so nefarious a business?'

It was dawning upon Crockett that this man was hardly what he had been led to expect. A puritan he might be, perhaps a crackpot, but he was committed as strongly to his principles in his fashion as Bart Ondane had been in his. Crockett rubbed his bruised arm.

'What you folks may decide to do with this business is your own affair, of course, since the three of you own it jointly. I was merely pointing out that it would be easy to dispose of it—'

'You mean sell it to others for a profit, while they in turn would take a profit from the tears of the widows and the fatherless?' August cut in. 'God keep me from being such a hypocrite! If indeed this place of debauchery be mine, then there shall be one less left to pollute the land, this very day! Set a match to it! Let the smoke of its burning be at least a partial atonement for the evil it has fostered!'

Crockett goggled. He had held Bart Ondane in a mixture compounded of fear, respect and a belated contempt, but he was far from sure that he did not prefer him to his brother-in-law.

'Burn it?' he repeated. 'But that would be criminal—impossible. Arson is a crime—'

'Is it not a crime to debauch your fellow-men? And when did it become a crime for a man to do with his own property as he may see fit?'

Crockett fumbled for a reply. He prided himself on his facility with words, since persuasion was a considerable part of his business. The angle of attack confused him.

'What I mean is, if you were to set fire to this structure, the blaze would spread to the buildings on either side, perhaps destroying the town. Such a course is impossible.'

Some of the glare faded from August's eyes as he confirmed that. The saloon was not like a shed on an isolated farm, to sink into its own ashes, affecting nothing else. Fire clearly was not the answer.

'The building's not at fault,' Nels observed, and August looked at him in surprise. 'It's the type of business conducted within its walls to which you object.'

August nodded. 'That is it,' he agreed. 'But to that I do more than object. I long since dedicated myself to the destruction of so nefarious an enterprise, whenever opportunity offered.'

He strode across the street, the others at his heels. Mary's cheeks were pale in the dusk, save for a spot of color in each. What was happening was beyond her wildest imaginings. It appeared that the newly kindled hope for the future seemed destined once again to go out, to vanish like the smoke of which August had spoken.

Still she was conscious of a thrill of pride. Whatever else he might or might not be, August was consistent.

He flung open the door of the saloon, standing to gaze about, his nose wrinkling at the odors of liquor and tobacco. Nels was on one side, Mary on the other, the lawyer a step behind. A look of mingled calculation and satisfaction was deep in Crockett's eyes.

Nels looked about with lively curiosity. He had been raised to respect his uncle's principles, and this was his first glimpse inside a saloon. Proof that it might be a money-maker was afforded by the considerable group gathered at the tables or along the bar. The glitter of bottles and glasses was impressive.

To August, the picture was neither new nor surprising. He had been inside many saloons, usually at the request of wives or relatives, to induce those for whom they were concerned to come away.

The customers, swelled in numbers by the curious who had followed them in, watched with curiosity and surprise as August strode to the bar. His presence was so commanding, his purpose so manifest that no one questioned his right. The bartender had just set out a quart bottle, and he looked uneasily beyond August to Crockett. At the lawyer's head-shake, he shrugged and stood back, offering no resistance as August snatched the bottle almost from the fingers of the man who had ordered it. Almost with the same gesture he flung it wildly, to break and shatter it against the far wall.

'There is the end!' he pronounced. 'So shall all this vile stuff be destroyed! No more of it shall be sold to men in this place, from this hour forth and forever! The business is closed.'

Most of the onlookers gaped in uneasy, uncomprehending silence. Only the man from whose grip the bottle had been so unceremoniously snatched risked a complaint. Physically he was big, though not particularly outstanding. It was his air which suggested importance. His face, already flushed, became congested.

'What's the big idea?' he demanded. 'That was my whiskey!'

'If you have paid for it, your money will be returned,' August informed him. 'No more liquor will be sold in this place.'

'Money?' the affronted man protested. 'Blast it, man, I don't want money. It's whiskey I crave—'

'So I understand, very well. The craving for the stuff is the ruin of men. I will not have the guilt of such ruination upon my soul!'

Rage inflamed the already reddened eyes so close to his own. This interloper mouthed words which made no sense. Worse, he was interfering with a man's right to buy and drink what he chose, and showing no contrition for such meddling.

'Out of my way!' The words were couched in a rising growl. 'Do you know who I am?'

A heady triumph was affecting August. For once he was important, acting the part he had so often dreamed.

'Who you are I know not; neither do I care. You are drunk—'

A roar bellowed up as from the lungs of a wounded grizzly, and the other man lashed out in blind fury. Few men had ever been able to stand up against Draine, and it did not occur to him that this one might. But rage, and the tendency of his vision to blur, made for miscalculation. His swing filled the air, lashing at emptiness. As he swayed, spinning half around, August closed big hands on his arms, below the shoulders. Whirling Draine about, he propelled him across the floor, and someone jerked open the door. With a tremendous heave, August sent Draine staggering halfway across the street, where he fell and slid.

Until that moment, Draine had been drunk. Now, in the reaction of rage, he was suddenly sobered, a coldly precise fighting machine. Even as he rolled to a stop, he was twisting about, grabbing, coming back to his feet with gun in hand.

CHAPTER FOUR

Though still staggering and uncertain as he came to his feet, Draine's motion with the gun was as smooth and deadly as the strike of a rattler. Then, with the gun in his hand half-raised, he checked the motion, staring at the man framed in the doorway—at the two men. Blinking, he looked again, and a film of fear spread across his eyes, dimming the haze of rage.

The man who had affronted him so grossly was there, an easy target. But the other man who had appeared out of nowhere, watching, was like a bad dream, or perhaps a nightmare.

'You!' Draine muttered. 'You're dead! Hang it, Ondane, you're dead!'

Terror had him in its grip. It was partly the result of too much liquor, so that he was far from cert.in who or what he saw. No man had ever accused Draine of cowardice, but this was too much. He swung about and plunged away into the night, forgetful of the gun he clutched.

Nels had moved instinctively to side his uncle, watching with a thrill of fear which gave way to amazement. August turned back, closing the door. The significance of the byplay had escaped him. For the moment, though he would have denied it indignantly, he was as drunk as Draine had been, with a heady triumph. Flushed with it, he was blind to all else.

His voice sounded almost normal, purged of anger. The brief fight, with its triumphant conclusion, had been like a tonic.

'I'm sorry, gentlemen,' he observed. 'Mr. Crockett informs me that this place and its contents belong to us, an inheritance from my wife's brother, Bart Ondane. Liquor in all its forms I find repugnant, and to sell it is against my principles; therefore this business is closed. If you will be so kind as to depart the premises, leaving the place to us, I will be grateful.'

Breaths had been sharply indrawn at the rude ejection of Draine, boss of the Axe. Knowing Draine, his proficiency with a gun and his swift rages, they had watched in horrified expectation. Then, spearheaded by Draine, their fascinated attention had shifted to Nels.

Ondane! It had been a name feared and respected as well as hated, and even without August's added confirmation, everyone could see now that an Ondane stood among them. If Draine had mistaken him for a man now dead, it was not too surprising. The resemblance, in that moment, was striking.

Remembering the ease with which August had thrown Draine through the door, the quelling of Draine's rage as he gazed at an Ondane, most of them obeyed the request, voicing no objection.

Only one man had the temerity to question the edict. He too had had a few too many drinks, and his mood was truculent.

'You mean you're going to destroy this—all this good whiskey?'

'I mean just that,' August agreed. Triumph was still a heady brew, which he had sipped but rarely. 'Liquor is an evil. The gutters will run with it.'

He stopped in amazement as Nels spoke, for the first time since entering the saloon.

'It will not be destroyed.'

August swung about in disbelief. Rarely did Nels dispute his decisions. A clash had been averted when the letter had arrived and all of them had determined to go West, rather than Nels alone. Never before had Nels openly contradicted him.

'What did you say?' he demanded.

'We will find a way to handle this without destroying what is here,' Nels explained. 'One third of it is mine,' he added. 'Another third belongs to Aunt Mary. Besides, there are other points to be considered.'

The man who had protested shrugged, then followed the others out into the night. Only one other outsider remained, aside from the lawyer. The bartender, after an uncertain look around, removed his apron and disappeared.

The man who waited had been one of the last to enter. A watch chain of gold nuggets, linked together, sagged across his vest. Aside from that, and a pronounced limp when he walked, there was nothing about him to attract attention.

August looked uncertain. Catching sight of the other man, he turned to him in relief.

'Did you want something, sir?' he asked.

'Why, now, that could be,' was the equable retort. 'I'm a business man, and I take it that you—all of you—are inclined the same way.'

Crockett interposed:

'Permit me, please. Mr. Ondane, and Mr. and Mrs. Millard, this is Mike Harris, who runs the other saloon.'

August stiffened, but he was almost past surprise.

'As a man, sir, you are welcome. But you'll understand that I have scant liking for your business.'

'You've made that abundantly clear,' Harris agreed dryly. 'I'm sure that Draine was surprised by the force of your argument.'

August refused to be beguiled. 'You said something about business?'

'I did. I take it that you do not care to run or even continue to own this business, since you find it distasteful. So it occurred to me that perhaps we might make a deal, to our mutual advantage. If you're going out of business, you'll want to be rid of this stock of liquor. It would be to my interest to buy what you have, rather than transport more in from a distance.'

August studied him with interest, not so much because of what Harris said as because of the way he said it.

'Pardon me for saying so, but you don't quite fit my notion of a man who would be in such a business.'

Harris shrugged. 'Meaning that I don't seem either a bum or a bloodsucker? All kinds and conditions of people inhabit this country—which surprises some.'

'I'm sure of that,' August agreed hastily. 'But do you think, sir, that I would be any less a hypocrite to refuse to sell such stuff direct, and then to have it reach the same throats, and the price for it still go into my pocket?'

Harris fingered his chin.

'You have a point, Mr. Millard. On the other hand, consider the other side of the question. Should you carry out your intention of smashing these bottles and emptying the casks into the street, you stand to lose a good part of your inheritance, to the value of several thousand dollars. Pouring whiskey into the gutter would be a spectacular gesture, but one which would return you not a single cent, nor do you any possible good. Nor would it affect others, either myself or any of my customers. I intend to continue in business. If you don't supply me, then I will buy elsewhere, and others will buy from me. That leaves you folks as the only losers.'

August was uncomfortably aware of his wife's gaze, and the already declared challenge of Nels. In this room was represented enough wealth to make the long-promised difference in their lives, or to leave them still in poverty. Such a situation seemed like a conspiracy, and it probably was, deliberately engineered by Bart Ondane. His tone quivered with resentment.

'I consider such a business to be debasing, sir, and utterly wrong. I oppose selling a product which hurts and degrades those who drink it, and making a profit from the misery of poor devils who, in the grip of a habit, cannot help themselves. How you may feel about it—'

He paused, flushing uncomfortably. 'I'm sorry.' Harris shrugged without resentment.

'You picture me, sir, as unfeeling and uncaring where my fellow beings are concerned. And you may be right. In my defense I can only observe that a horse threw me, some years ago, causing injuries so that I could no longer make a living as I had been accustomed to do. So some of my friends and neighbors got together and very generously set me up in this business, which I could manage. You have a wife and nephew. I am not so fortunate, but I do have a daughter to support.

'There is also the certainty that if I don't sell the stuff, men will buy it from someone else. That may be a poor reason and no real justification, but it is the situation.'

August regarded him with increasing wonder. He found the argument unsettling and confusing.

'Wouldn't I still be a hypocrite?' he asked.

'As I am? It seems to me, sir, that there are degrees of hypocrisy, just as there are shades between black and white. To this extent I'll go along with you. Some aspects of the business, and certain of its effects upon some men, I heartily dislike. If by closing the doors of my saloon, too, together we could insure that no other would operate in this part of the country, I would seriously consider doing so.

'Money-wise, that would hit me hard, as it might you, but it would perhaps be worth it. On the other hand, I don't know that either of us have the right to set ourselves up as judges over our fellow-men, to regulate their conduct according to our ideas rather than theirs. In any case, it would be an empty gesture, and completely futile.'

He waved an encompassing hand.

'The law permits the sale, so other men, with no scruples, would have new saloons opened and operating within a very few days. No one would be helped, no problems solved.

That being so, I expect to continue in business, and I thought that it might be mutually helpful to buy your stock. So think it over. Then, later, if you are so minded, we can discuss it further.'

He bowed to Mary, nodded to Nels and the lawyer, and let himself out. August found himself at a loss. Life was not nearly so simple as he had believed.

'I don't like it,' he protested. 'It's not fair, such a situation. Not fair at all. I had supposed that this would be a ranch—'

Crockett interposed, rubbing his hands briskly.

'You folks must be all tired out,' he said. 'There are rooms above stairs for living quarters, which belonged to Mr. Ondane. They are yours now, of course, and they have been cleaned and readied for your use. You'll probably want to cook some supper. You'll find supplies, everything you'll need. I'll see you tomorrow.'

With a lamp, they climbed the outer stairs. Mary gave a little gasp of pleasure. These rooms had been a man's, but when it came to a place to live, Bart Ondane had liked his comfort. The whole upper floor was given over to living quarters, a kitchen, bedrooms, parlor and dining room. A far later and better model of range than she had ever owned was in the kitchen. Cupboards were handy, stocked with all sorts of supplies. Best of all, especially as this was on the second floor, a spring from the nearby hills had been piped down and into the saloon, the pipe running up into the kitchen. Clear cold water flowed steadily, conveniently at hand, the overflow going out again.

With Nels assisting, a meal was quickly prepared. August sat in thought, but he already knew what the decision had to be. There could be a jut to Mary's chin, and she was, after all, an Ondane. She and Nels had a two-thirds interest—

He would have been surprised at Nels' train of thought. Such matters, while important, were trivial by comparison. Why were they there? Certainly not because Bart had been anxious to make amends. The answer was apt to contain more surprises, as joltingly unexpected as the saloon had been.

CHAPTER FIVE

His aunt and uncle were still sleeping when Nels descended to the street the next morning. It had been a strange homecoming, if this place was to be their home or could be called by such a name. August was frustrated and bewildered. Nels' emotions differed, but he was anxious to find out what they had gotten into.

At this hour the town was virtually deserted. The exception was a girl, who came around the corner of the rival saloon, leading a saddled horse. She wore a shirt open at the neck and a man's hat, wide-brimmed and far from new, atop a pile of soft brown hair. A pair of field-glasses were slung from a case over her shoulder. Taken by surprise, Nels stared. Becoming aware of it, he colored, jerking off his hat.

'Good morning—er, excuse me,' he stammered. 'I didn't mean to be rude—'

Her answer was a smile which confirmed his first impression. She was not merely pretty, but almost bewitchingly so. Somehow he hadn't expected to find such a girl in such a town.

'A girl likes to be noticed,' she returned matter-of-factly, and studied him in return with frank appraisal. 'You're Nels Ondane, aren't you?'

'Yes,' he agreed. Apparently the news concerning them had spread fast. His uncle's impassioned declaration regarding liquor and the saloon would be on every tongue.

'I'm Janie Harris,' she explained. 'So we're neighbors. And new neighbors are rather rare in this country.' Without saying whether that was good or not, she mounted swiftly, controlling her impatient horse to study him a moment longer. 'In any case, you're welcome,' she added, then was down the street and out on to the road, where it led off to the widening valley to the south, at a run.

Nels watched while she disappeared, suddenly realizing that there were a lot of questions which he'd like to ask; it would have been pleasant to talk a little longer. She must be the daughter of Mike Harris, and his notions, like those of August, required some readjustment. If Mike Harris was hardly his idea of a saloon-keeper, Janie was even less what he'd expect a saloon man's daughter to be.

Mockery could be surveyed almost at a glance, and outwardly at least it seemed to conceal no other surprises. He turned down the road, walking aimlessly. It would probably be possible to get a horse and ride, but that could come later. For a man accustomed to using his own legs, he'd been too cooped up on train and stage. He wanted to be alone, to study what he'd learned and what he surmised.

With a fair distance to lend perspective, the mountains on every side loomed tall and massive, the valley between widening until it looked like an empire. The Valley of the Gun! This had been Bart Ondane's country, and in that connection, the name seemed appropriate. There was a creek on either side of the road, each stream seeming to disdain the other turning to east and west. They were symbolic of the men who inhabited the valley.

The stage driver had told him something of the situation here, of its explosive potentialities. Seven sheep outfits occupied the main or middle part of the valley, and they were hemmed in and surrounded by an equal number of cattle ranches which, crowded onto less choice and more rugged terrain, watched enviously. An uneasy truce had prevailed for a long while, but the driver had hinted that long-smoldering resentments were likely to erupt at any time.

That being the case, the coming of another Ondane to the valley, and the seemingly irrational behavior of his uncle might prove just the factors needed to trigger violence. Had Bart, with his long-held sense of wrong and twisted sense of humor, planned it that way?

Nels shook his head impatiently. The notion didn't make sense. Nonetheless, it persisted.

A wheel-trace swung toward the west, and he followed that, finding himself among a cluster of low hills, the town shut away. A flat stone offered an inviting seat, and the early sun was pleasantly warm. He moved toward it, but checked at a sound of voices.

Three men came around the hill, also on foot. They were young, all being about his own age. They came on, moving purposefully, clearly not surprised at seeing him. A warning bell rang in his mind, the certainty that this was no chance encounter.

They must have seen him set out from town, then followed. He was partly reassured to see that none of them was armed, at least outwardly, but neither was he. And that might have been a mistake.

The town was close at hand, but from the wildness of the country, one would never guess its presence; nor did it necessarily betoken either civilization or safety. In this valley, the name of Ondane would probably be no passport to friendship.

In one way, this encounter was nothing new, but similar to some he had experienced on other occasions when they had moved to a new community. At the outset, there was always hostility from other kids. For that reason, he'd had his share of fights. Yet this was somehow different.

Two of the three he took to be brothers, thick-set and stockily built, their hair carroty-red and overlong. The third was taller, his hair the tint of fresh straw, with eyes of a matching paleness. Somehow, Nels was reminded of a crouching puma.

They halted, eying him with mingled derision and barely veiled animosity.

'So *this* is what we get for an addition to the community,' the tall boy observed. He spat. '*Chechaco*!'

The word was new to Nels, but it was clearly intended to be derogatory. The brothers laughed, as if on cue.

'He's sure got tender feet, all right. And from his looks, he's a Scowegian, to boot!'

They laughed uproariously, and Nels felt his ears begin to burn. He waited, watchfully silent.

'Scowegians are no darn good!' one of the brothers observed.

'Oh, a Swede or maybe a Norsk ain't so bad,' his brother contradicted. 'But when you get one named Ondane, that's different.'

'I'll say it is,' the tall boy chimed in. 'We've had too many Ondanes already.' He addressed Nels directly. 'What'd you come here for?'

'I guess you know why I came,' Nels returned, and was about to add more, but was checked by another cackle of laughter.

'Oh, sure, we know why you came, all right! Old Bart left his saloon to you folks! And ain't that something to make the devil giggle, leavin' a saloon to a temperance man, who thinks whiskey's twice as poisonous as the bite of a rattler!'

Nels waited alertly. There was no doubt that they had followed him out here, looking for trouble. The mirth directed at Bart Ondane and the saloon no longer bothered him, not in view of the memory of Janie Harris, and her fresh, wind-swept look. Somehow, those few moments with her had changed a lot of things, even long-cherished opinions.

As though he were a mind-reader, the tall boy blurted out her name, suddenly belligerent.

'You get one thing straight to start with, Ondane. I ain't scared of you on account of your name or what happened last night—and Janie Harris is my girl! So you keep away from her!'

So that was the reason for this. Nels was both surprised and disgusted. The surprise was that so pretty a girl would have anything to do with so pale an imitation of a man, coupled with annoyance at the implied threat. He shrugged.

'If that's what's worrying you, forget it. I don't even know her.'

'Oh, yeah? Weren't you talkin' with her already this morning?'

'I suppose I was, but she spoke to me. First time I ever saw her.'

That was so obviously true that it left them at a loss, but not for long. One of the brothers had a new idea.

'Oh, so she ain't good enough for the likes of an Ondane, is that it? Her old man runs a saloon, but you and *your* old man wouldn't sully your lips with a drink of the stuff, would you?'

'Whiskey's good enough for *men*,' his brother chimed in promptly. 'That's what folks drink out here, real tarantula juice. Bet you've never even had a taste, have you?'

Again, they gave him no opportunity to reply, advancing suddenly, closing in from all sides. The tall boy suddenly had a pint flask in one hand, and Nels began to understand why they had followed him, the clever notion which he supposed had come to them when they had seen him leave town alone. It was typical that they should figure that it would be a huge joke to make him take a drink. They could boast that the nephew of the teetotaler, of tough old Bart Ondane, liked the whiskey which his uncle scorned.

He'd be a laughing stock, and so would August. Bart Ondane was dead, but whatever heritage he had left for the valley was not only moving; it was beginning to accelerate. Such a thing as this, coming at this time, would help to further its advance.

'If you ain't, then it's time you had a good swig,' the pale-eyed man observed, and if he thought like a prankish youth, he was older and hard in purpose. 'Then when you talk about drinking, you'll have some notion what you're gabbin' about!'

'What makes you think I've never had a drink?' Nels countered.

The question disconcerted them, as he had intended, since it was so much at variance with what they were prepared for. He made use of their pause to jump and grab. If he could get the flask and smash it, there would still be a fight, but there would no danger any longer of being forced to drink. Angry at their taunts, he rather welcomed a fight.

His ruse almost worked. His fingers closed on the bottle, but the tall boy, alarmed, jerked back; then they were struggling fiercely, silently, for its possession. Then the others took a hand, clearly having no scruples about fair play. Having expected that, Nels was ready for them.

He lashed out with one foot, kicking backward, as one brother jumped him from behind, the other lunging in from the side. At three to one, Nels saw no reason for observing the niceties which they scorned. Luck was aided by speed. His foot caught one man in the stomach, knocking him sprawling. He lay gasping, then recovered enough to double up, groaning and clutching at his middle.

His brother had better luck, a wild grab catching Nels' hair. He jerked, wrenching savagely, as though to twist Nels' head from his shoulders. Then the three of them were down, locked together, rolling and kicking, in as wildly desperate a melee as Nels had ever known. Somewhat grudgingly, Nels revised his earlier opinion. For all the paleness of his eyes and hair, the tall kid was as tough as his companions, and just as short on scruples.

It was becoming apparent to them that they'd caught a tartar. Three to one, they had looked for an easy conquest. They would intimidate him, make him taste the whiskey, and that would be enough for their present purpose.

But this Ondane was as redoubtable in one respect as his uncle had been; he knew how to fight. Except for their anger, and the humiliation of accepting defeat at such odds, they would have cut and run.

Sudden added weight driving down on his back warned Nels that the other brother had regained his wind and was adding his impetus to the contest, getting in a lick wherever an opportunity was offered. A hard-driven boot missed his ribs, but raked painfully along a thigh. Choked, half-blinded, Nels fought doggedly.

The one man's judgment was still somewhat impaired by the blow he had first taken. His fingers found a rock beneath his hand. Sensing what it was, his fingers closed eagerly; then he smashed with it in a hammering motion, aiming for the back of Nels' head. He missed his intended target, the rock scraping instead along the skull of the tall man. He went limp at its smash, legs buckling. For an instant, frightened at what he had done, the wielder of the rock contemplated flight.

Then, seeing his friend stir, he lashed out again as Nels heaved about. This time the blow was better aimed, and Nels collapsed in turn.

The three got to their feet, breathing hard, the tall man last of all. Glaring, they took stock. The proneness of Nels Ondane was cause for satisfaction, but only for a moment. He was much too white, too still. Allowing the rock to fall from uncertain fingers, its wielder gasped.

'He ain't dead, is he?'

'No thanks to you if he ain't. What'd you want to do a thing like that for?' The tall man stooped, then straightened, relieved. 'Naw, he's just knocked out.'

He seized an arm, shaking Nels roughly. There was no result, and his own face took on a look of apprehension, then cleared.

'We'll bring him around, and sort of kill two birds with one club, eh? Watch.'

He retrieved the flask, which he had managed to toss to one side as the struggle grew hot. Twisting out the cork, he spilled liquor over Nels' face, so that some ran into his partly opened mouth. Nels choked and gasped, showing signs of returning consciousness.

'What'd I tell you? He'll come around.' Hastily the tall man emptied the remaining contents of the flask over Nels' face and shirt. Then, tossing the empty bottle onto the grass beside him, the trio hastily decamped.

CHAPTER SIX

August, upon awakening, was still confused and uncertain, a state of mind which he resented. Usually he had no trouble making decisions, justifying them on the grounds that a thing was either right or wrong. However unpalatable the course, that was all that mattered.

Now, looking about the pleasant rooms on the top floor, he knew that this was not so simple a situation. Here was a finer house than he'd ever known before, the sort that he'd so glibly promised Mary on many occasions in their earlier years of married life. She liked it, and that must be taken into consideration.

The added knowledge that Bart Ondane had planned for things to work out this way, laughing as he carried out a long-cherished revenge, made it worse.

August Millard lived by a rigid standard, and his principles admitted of no deviation from it. Liquor, as he more than once had been able to observe, could be detrimental to its users; therefore it was to be destroyed rather than tolerated. In the abstract, that had been simple and clear-cut.

All at once, he was part-owner of a store of liquor worth thousands of dollars, and suddenly it was no longer simple or easy. Mike Harris had been plausible in making the argument that destruction of the liquor would be an empty gesture, changing nothing—except that it would leave August's pockets as empty as they habitually were.

There was the rub. The straightness of Mary's back as she went about preparing breakfast was eloquent. Her principles were as high as his own, but her notions of the practical did not always jibe with his. In addition, Bart Ondane was her brother. Though she disapproved as strongly of his ways, that influenced her reasoning. These bottled goods represented a lot of money—wealth such as August had many times assured her would soon be theirs, now tangibly within reach for the first time.

She and Nels were legally owners of a controlling interest. Nels had also pointed out that such an act of destruction, which most people would regard as not merely wasteful but criminal, might trigger violence in the valley.

A worn plank walk ran for a couple of blocks on either side of the street. Next to that, the hitch-rail in front of the Powdersmoke Saloon was chewed and splintery, and on this a man leaned as August descended to the street. The loiterer, who was formed after the pattern of a bale of hay, regarded him expectantly, without shifting position. His hair was in need of cutting, though he was freshly shaven, and for all its whiteness, the thatch showed no sign of thinning. Eyes as blue as the sky held a matching blandness.

'A beautiful day in the morning,' he observed, as August halted at the foot of the stairway. Casually he added. 'M' name's O'Mara.'

He extended a hand, once well calloused, and still firm and hard. August took it.

'It is a fine day,' he agreed. 'If you're waiting for the saloon to open, it won't.'

'Not me.' O'Mara lounged across to the building, cocking a foot comfortably against the side. 'I heard what happened last night. Such news gets around.'

'I suppose it does. I suppose you're thinking that I made a fool of myself?'

'Not me,' O'Mara denied. 'A man's business is his own, or at least it ought to be. But then, I'm old enough to take a broad view, or I like to think I do, especially when something don't affect me one way or the other. I've always noticed that it's a mighty sight easier to be philosophical, when it ain't your mule that's balking.'

'I suppose you're right . . . You knew my brother-in-law?'

'Bart? Sure did.' O'Mara gazed blandly at the sun. 'I take it that you're still aimin' to close the saloon?'

'It's closed. For good.'

'Fine with me. Only that could make a lot of trouble, for you and for others.'

'How do you mean?'

'Oh, there are plenty of ways. People get notions. Some sort of feel that they have certain rights, where maybe they really don't. Squatters' rights, I suppose you'd call it.'

It was approaching the middle of the morning, for, tired from the long journey by rail and road, they had overslept. Others were on the street now, some pausing within earshot, as though hoping to hear what might be said. A hawk soared above the town. August jerked his thoughts back to what O'Mara was saying.

'Squatters' rights?'

'In a manner of speaking. Let a man, any man, camp long enough, and he sort of gets a notion that the land he's on belongs to him. It's the same with folks who've have been patronizin' this saloon for years. A lot of them weren't too partial to the man that owned it, but they traded here, one reason being that he stocked mighty good liquor. After buyin' that for so long, they figure that they've a sort of vested interest in the place.'

That was understandable. August remembered the closing of a store where he had liked to trade. It had been sold to make way for a new enterprise, and he had hated to see it go.

'You're getting at something, Mr. O'Mara. What?'

'You're a more direct man than your brother-in-law. He had a way of circling wide to achieve an objective. Too much abruptness can lead to misunderstandings. What I'm trying to point out is that, whether folks liked Bart or not, they liked his saloon. Some, not all. Now they've no place to go, all at once.'

'There's still Harris' place.' August jerked a thumb.

'Sure, sure, only it ain't quite the same. Maybe they will go there if they have to. But some would take it hard if you poured out a lot of good liquor into the dust or smashed the bottles. It would strike them as a sinful waste.'

'What about pouring poison down a man's throat?' August countered heatedly. 'It seems to me that what I choose to do with my own property is nobody's business but my own.'

'Opinions differ. Then there's the matter of cattle and sheep.'

'Cattle and sheep? I'm afraid I don't understand.'

'Bart Ondane ran cattle, so naturally the cattlemen patronized the Powdersmoke. The sheepmen, on the other hand, all drank at Harris' place. It got to be sort of a habit—almost a tradition. And one benefit was, it kept them apart.'

'I still don't see—'

'You're new here, or you would. It could be a fighting matter, if there was only one place for everybody to go for a drink.'

'My contention, Mr. O'Mara, is that one need not drink at all. None of my family ever touch the stuff—'

August broke off, staring in disbelief. Others were looking also, as Nels came walking slowly, his gait uncertain. His eyes were bloodshot, and he looked as though he had been wallowing on the ground. He staggered, despite all efforts to hold himself steady. Worse, as he came nearer, there was the unmistakable reek of whiskey.

August had seen drunkenness too many times to mistake the symptoms. It was beyond credence, almost beyond belief, that Nels should be drunk at this hour of the morning. Still, he had stolen away before they were up, and he could have helped himself to a bottle—

'Nels!' Shock rang loud in August's voice. 'What has happened?'

Nels halted, leaning against the side of the building as O'Mara had just been doing. His head was clearing, though it still throbbed painfully, and there was a large and very sore lump where the rock had pounded. His legs still had a tendency to wobble, though not so badly as when he had forced them to head back to town. Somewhat hazily he realized that it might have been better to rest awhile, to regain his wits and strength before setting out, but he had been too dazed to think clearly.

'I—I—' He began. Then the words slurred and his tongue faltered. August was outraged.

'You've been drinking,' he charged. 'You're drunk!'

Nels shook his head in denial. The motion was painful, but he persisted stubbornly.

'I'm not drunk,' he protested. 'Some fellows—three of them—tried to make me take a drink. Then I—I don't remember just what happened—'

He broke off, looking where others were watching. The three who had jumped him were coming along the road, moving with an air of careless innocence, approaching from the opposite end of the town. This appeared to them to be the right moment for more fun, for frosting the cake.

'Here's where we cash in on the fruits of our labor,' the tall man observed to his companions.

'Those are the fellows,' Nels said, 'the ones that tried to make me take a drink.'

'It looks as though they did more than try,' August returned, but his anger was beginning to shift, as he saw that Nels must be telling the truth. Of his own accord he would hardly drink enough to be in such a state so early in the day. 'No need to lie about it.'

'I'm not lying.' Stung, Nels straightened,

anger helping to clear his head. 'We had a fight. Then I don't remember just what happened—'

A crowd was gathering, attracted as much by those who were involved as by the promise of excitement. The three instigators halted at the edge of the group, grinning derisively.

'What on earth is he talking about?' the tall man asked, looking blankly at his companions. 'He looks as though he'd spent the night in a hog pen, and he smells like a saloon, but what does he mean about us?'

Both brothers shook their heads. 'Reckon there's a mistake somewhere. It can't be us he's meaning. This is the first time we ever set eyes on him.'

'They're lying,' Nels protested angrily. 'They tried to make me take a drink, and when I wouldn't, all three of them jumped me.'

His own condition seemed to lend some verification to the statement, but theirs disproved the charge. None of them had taken much outward punishment in the struggle. Having brushed their clothes and eradicated such signs as had been visible, they had returned to town. The tall man was indignant.

'From the way it looks, he went off by himself to do some drinking, and not being used to it, I suppose, he had too much and got soused. So now he wants to put the blame on somebody else. So far as we're concerned, we've been together all morning, up north of town.'

His companions nodded confirmation. It was three to one, and Nels understood how they were working it, and that his condition was against him. The dizziness from the blow on the head rocked him anew, and he clasped his head miserably.

'I tell you they're lying,' he insisted. 'My head's splitting.'

August looked about, perplexed. It was doubly shocking that Nels, who had always been steady and dependable, should so far yield to temptation as to slip out early, taking a bottle, and go off to get so drunk that he could not even talk straight. The symptoms of a hangover from which he seemed to be suffering were only what was to be expected.

Also, it was the testimony of three to one, and the trio had come from the opposite direction. The onlookers were viewing the evidence with frank disgust.

'Get upstairs,' August ordered, 'if you're able to climb them. I'll deal with you later—'

He jerked back at a sudden pounding of hoofs as a rider swept up, almost overwhelming him before stopping in a small cloud of dust. The rider gazed about, her cheeks holding a red hue of fury. Though she was too far away to hear, she had no difficulty guessing what had been said.

'Don't you believe your own nephew?' she demanded of August. 'You should. You ought to be proud of him, a man like he is! He's telling the truth.'

The trio were staring with bewilderment and dismay. 'How do you know?' August countered, willing to be convinced, but more confused than ever.

'I know because I saw the whole thing! They tried to make him take a drink, then hammered him with a stone and left him for dead—'

The tall man interrupted hastily.

'What on earth are you talking about, Janie? How could you have seen? There was nobody anywhere around—'

He checked and clapped a hand to his mouth, reddening at the realization that his words were a betrayal. Janie's glance burned through him.

'So you admit it, Larch Draine! You might as well, for I saw the whole thing.' She swung her field-glasses aloft for everyone to see. 'I was too far away to do anything about it, but I'd been watching an eagle through these, and then I saw the three of you stalking him, and watched. It was as brutal and disgraceful a thing as I ever saw,' she added to the onlookers, 'three of them jumping one man. Yet I believe that he'd have whipped all of you put together, if you'd fought fair—'

She broke off, then abruptly was out of the

saddle, running across to Nels, setting an arm about his shoulders as he staggered. Blinding nausea gripped him again, so that he would have gone down without her support. She steered him toward the stairway, where she was joined by Mary, who came hastening down the steps. Together they helped him climb.

CHAPTER SEVEN

After witnessing the assault, Janie Harris had lost no time. It had been pure chance that she had picked them out in the field-glasses when she had, but knowing the trio as she did, she had guessed instantly that they were up to no good. She had gritted her teeth in helpless rage while the lenses brought distant objects within easy viewing distance. There were miles to cover in actual riding, with a long, deep gorge which would have to be circled around, rather than crossed.

So it had been impossible to help. When they had slunk away, leaving Nels lying as though dead, she had jumped on her horse and set out for town again, taking the necessarily long course to go to Nels' aid first. Occasionally she had used her glasses to keep track of the three, observing how they circled to come into town from the opposite direction. Nels had recovered sufficiently to make a staggering return before she reached the spot. He had fallen a couple of times while she was still well behind, but had struggled up and kept going, eliciting her admiration.

'He put up a grand fight!' she told Mary proudly. 'Had they fought at all fair, I've no doubt but what he'd have beaten all three of them, and sure they must have figured the same! One used a rock to hit him with, so that he went down as though pole-axed, and I was terrified that he was dead.

'I'm glad to have them shown up for the cowards they are!' she added vehemently. 'That Larch Draine has walked so long in the shadow of his father that he thinks he's a man himself, and the Van Sickles do whatever he says!'

'Draine?' Mary echoed. 'Was that not the man who—last night—'

'The same,' Janie agreed. 'Your husband threw him out, and everybody's still wondering that he's alive this morning to walk abroad! Draine owns the Axe, the big cattle ranch which runs right up to the edge of town, off to the south and west. Most people are afraid of the Lumbartons and terrified of the Draines.'

But not you, Mary thought, watching the girl. Certainly not you. Her own emotions bewildered her. She was frightened, yet curiously exhilarated, even determined. It must be that she was more like her brother, even to an unguessed wild streak, than she had ever supposed. Aloud she said:

'Will this cause more trouble? Perhaps Mr. Draine will resent the fact that his son has been made to appear foolish before so many.'

'He'll not like it,' Janie agreed. 'They've been spoiling for trouble,' she added soberly. 'It looks as though they figured that this gave them a good excuse for starting some.'

'And these others—the Van Sickles?'

'Their father owns the Box B, off at the southeast corner of the valley. The three boys run together. It's a funny thing,' she added with wrinkling brow. 'Those two have been cosyin' up to the sheepmen lately, and so has Larch. That don't make sense.'

Nels, stretched on a coach, listened with closed eyes, perforce because of a wet cloth held over them. Janie's touch seemed to ease the throbbing. He felt a little foolish, but on the whole it was pleasant to be fussed over in such a fashion.

* * *

The onlookers drifted away. August let himself into the saloon and stood looking about appraisingly. It was a big place, well stocked, with a lot of money represented; money tied up in a product to encourage the debauchery of his fellow-men. He believed that, implicitly. Therefore, having the opportunity, he should destroy it.

On the other hand, it was not only property, but theirs, and its possession meant riches for the first time in his life. And Mary was involved, which made it doubly difficult.

She had been patient and long-suffering, awaiting a better day. This could be it. Should he destroy what had fallen to them, there would probably never be another chance. And yet—

This girl who had spoken up for Nels apparently was the daughter of Mike Harris, who ran the other saloon. It was on her account that Harris, unable to follow his usual line of work, had accepted the gift of a saloon and followed such a profession. For such a girl to spring from that kind of a background—

Everything was wrong, badly askew. Or could it be that the trouble was with himself? He turned with resolution and marched across to the Harris' place.

Mike was alone as he entered, mopping an already spotless bar. He turned courteously.

'Good morning to you, Mr. Millard. You look troubled.'

'I'm more than troubled,' August confessed. 'Did you notice what happened here a short while ago?' Finding that Mike did not he recounted events as he knew them.

'Your daughter is now with my wife and nephew. I am proud—but confused, not at all certain. Such events are completely outside my experience. I hardly know what to think.'

Harris nodded understandingly. 'I often find myself in the same fix,' he admitted. 'Life is seldom as simple as it seems it ought to be. As for the liquor—you would not run a saloon?'

'I could not.'

'Yet you have a stock of liquor, and I must buy more. If you destroy it, you lose, with no one else being affected—except that its destruction might trigger more trouble in this valley. Of course, if you sell to me, I stand to gain.'

Somewhat to his surprise, August found himself liking this man. He came to an abrupt decision.

'I don't know whether it's the right thing or not, but we'll sell it to you,' he decided. 'That is, if Nels and my wife are agreeable. The building can be used for other purposes.'

'Now there's a sensible solution,' Harris approved, 'one which should jibe with your conscience. As you say, the building can be put to some other use.'

'There must be room for other kinds of businesses.' August's ready enthusiasm was beginning to soar. 'Some sort of a well-equipped store, perhaps, should fill a real need.'

'I'm sure of it,' Harris agreed, but tugged at the lobe of his left ear. 'In ridding yourself of a problem, you're presenting me with one,' he added.

'What do you mean?'

'As you probably know by now, we have two groups or factions here in The Valley of the Gun. There are an equal number of sheep and cattle ranches. For both sides to have to get their liquor at one place—'

'You said something about that last evening. But surely it can't present a serious problem?'

'On the contrary. This is a big valley—mammoth, in fact. Each of the fourteen outfits is big. The country is peculiar in that the only good route in or out from it lies through this narrow canyon here at the northern apex, with Mockery sitting astride it. So all supplies come in and go out by this road, except for a few weeks in summer. So everybody, sheepmen and cattlemen alike, trade here. Until now, the town has been a sort of neutral ground, and respected as such. But making such a shift, forcing them to come together—'

'If a man serves the public fairly and impartially, no one has any right to complain.'

'That's a nice philosophy,' Harris conceded. 'But men who hate think with hearts and guns—not with their heads.'

CHAPTER EIGHT

Nels rode with a sense of unreality. He had recovered quickly from the effects of the beating, then, at his own suggestion, had set out for Highcard, half a hundred miles away, beyond the confines of the wide-reaching Valley of the Gun. The chief provision of Bart Ondane's will, in leaving them the heritage of the saloon, had been that a headstone should be erected above his grave, in his memory, with no undue delay.

In one sense it seemed a strange request, but in another it was understandable. Bart Ondane had been a power in the valley, a man of influence. But it was becoming unmistakably plain he had left behind a heritage of hate, that respect had been born of fear, not love.

Probably he had realized that if a marker was to be erected in his memory, once he was gone, he must make provision for it in advance. That he had done, and the sooner the obligation was fulfilled and out of the way, the better.

Since he'd headed off beyond his own range and died there, it would be a long, tiring journey. Circling by stagecoach, north out of the pass from Mockery and around, would double its length. Nels proposed to go by horse, down through the valley and out of the southern pass, then, his task completed, return the same way.

Mary had demurred, pointing out the vastness of the land, the loneliness, the risks. August had been all for it, and Nels was a man. So it had been agreed.

Aside from his aunt and uncle, he had confided his intention only to Janie Harris. Somehow it seemed natural to mention it to her, and he'd been glad of the impulse when he'd seen the quick concern in her eyes. She had voiced no objections, but had offered certain suggestions, drawing him a map of the valley with a stick in the dirt.

'It's a big country, and if you pick your course, you can probably ride all through it and never meet anyone else,' Janie explained seriously. 'Which might be better all around. There's a road runs roughly down the middle, and another angles south towards the western range of hills, but you might do better to stay off them. The sheepmen have never had any love for an Ondane, and after your clash with some of the sons of the cattlemen—'

Nels understood and appreciated the point. He wasn't scared, but prudence was only reasonable. A coiled lariat was tied at one side of his saddle, a coiled black-snake at the other. Either, properly used, could be an effective weapon. In addition, though he had not mentioned this to August or his aunt, he had purchased a six-gun and cartridge belt. It might come in handy, in a country where wild game was plentiful. And in this country, every man went armed as a matter of course.

He had picked out a good horse, and Janie's directions for reaching Highcard had seemed adequate. He would swing southwest through the big valley, out at the southern pass, then turn north by a little west, toward a mountain known as Baldy. It dominated the country beyond the valley, its snow-capped crest clearly visible. Highcard was somewhere near its foot.

He had followed Janie's advice, keeping prudently out of sight down through the valley. He'd sighted ranch buildings a couple of times, and riders on as many more occasions, but none of them had spotted him. The vastness of the valley, the mammoth upshoot of the surrounding mountains, had awed and impressed him at the same time filling him with a sense of exhilaration. He could understand why Bart Ondane had chosen to live in such a land.

In wildly remote country he'd tried out the gun, picking a target, making a fast draw, emptying the chamber within a reasonable distance of where the bullets were intended to go. One summer, a couple of years before, a neighboring farmer had allowed Nels to use his revolver, giving him some pointers. At least he hadn't forgotten the feel or how to use it.

By night he picketed his horse, then cooked provisions over a small fire. Those were skills he'd picked up on overnight camping trips in the Alleghenies. It was only when he rolled in a blanket that lonesomeness overcame him, enhanced during the first night by the uneasy snorting of his horse. Some animal was prowling, but he was not unduly worried until he spied the tracks the next morning, where it had watched the camp. A bear, he decided, and a big one.

It was afternoon of the day after he'd left the mountain barrier and headed toward Baldy when he felt some uneasiness, wondering if he was lost. For the past hour he had been unable to see even the shining crest of the big hill, which was both disquieting and hard to understand. The mountain should be straight on ahead.

The difficulty was the roughness of the country through which he journeyed. There were no roads there, no trails, no houses. As in the Valley of the Gun, the hills were high and the valleys deep, with a disconcerting fashion of twisting about. The evergreens which turned the hills blue at a distance showed almost black close at hand, like a shroud.

It might be well to climb a hill and get his bearings again. There had been a lot of twists and turns because of the terrain.

At that juncture he came upon the track of a shod horse. The sight was reassuring, yet vaguely disquieting. Reassuring, in that the sign was the first evidence of any other human being that he had seen that day. A shod horse would be ridden by someone. It was disturbing to find such sign where it might mean a prospector, but, just as likely, an outlaw.

'Reckon I am a *chechaco*,' he reflected glumly. He had asked Janie the meaning of the word, returning her grin when she'd explained that it meant tenderfoot. Right now he felt like one.

A closer look convinced him that the sign was nothing to feel either apprehensive or very hopeful about. Only eyes as keen as his would have noticed it at all. The tracks were far from fresh, perhaps weeks old.

Since the trail of the pony headed in the direction in which he believed he should go, Nels followed it, finding both a challenge and a sense of accomplishment in being able to read such scant sign. He went on for more than a mile, then made a discovery which surprised him. All at once the sign was fresh.

He puzzled over that, studying additional tracks, deciding that they had all been made by the same animal. A quarter of a mile farther on, he came upon a horse grazing in a small hidden meadow.

The cayuse was dun-colored, and it lifted

its head and whickered welcomingly at sight of another horse, then came trotting up. It was clearly lonesome, with a vague uneasiness to match his own. Examining it more closely, Nels was puzzled that it should be there, without rope, hobbles or bridle. The pony was free to move as it pleased, but it seemed to be lingering in that particular section of country.

Studying the terrain with care, he made out what looked like a tumble-down cabin at the edge of the meadow. It was all but hidden among brush and trees. The horse followed as he rode for a closer look, and his scalp prickled with a sense of disquiet for which he could find no reason.

The trees and brush had grown up since the cabin had been built, and it had the dilapidated look of long desertion. Only a new growth of weeds about the doorway had been trampled and crushed. The door had been hinged originally with two stout strips of leather. The lower of these had rotted, but the upper still held the door at a crazy angle. Nels pushed it open and looked in, trying to see in the gloom.

The first thing which he made out was a saddle on the floor near the door, a bridle and saddle-blanket draped over it. Then he made out other objects, one a bunk, built against the opposite wall. It looked broken and far from inviting, but in it was a man.

Nels' first impression was that the man was dead. He lay, sprawled in an uncomfortable fashion, while a fly circled restlessly about the room. Closer examination, after forcing his unwilling legs forward, did not quite confirm the first guess, though very nearly. The man was alive, but barely so.

He was big, bearded, with the look of a cowboy or ranchman, and he had been shot. The bullet had struck him in the back, plowing below his right shoulder and coming out in front, narrowly missing the lung, or so Nels judged, because the victim was still alive. Either it had been a heavy caliber or fired from close range. It had made an ugly wound, which had been crudely self-bandaged, a considerable accomplishment. Having been a hunter all his life, Nels could guess how much it must have bled, the weakening effect.

Somehow the injured man had survived, probably having had some food in a pack; also, there was water conveniently close, a small spring just beyond the cabin. It was easy to deduce that he had come there, perhaps intending to spend the night in the cabin, unsaddling. After that, undoubtedly from ambush, the bullet had come.

Apparently the killer had figured he was dead, and seen no need for a second shot.

The injured man had been too badly hurt, as well as too weak, to try and ride out for help. He had clung to life, apparently growing weaker with each passing day, yet, because of an innate stubbornness coupled with vitality, was taking a long time dying. Judging not only from the disordered cabin, but also from the look of the wound and the tracks of the horse, he must have been here for a good many days, perhaps even a few weeks.

That might account for the cayuse remaining close by, in an instinct of loyalty to its rider. Apparently no one else had come anywhere near after the departure of the gunman.

It was sheer chance that Nels had come there, on his way toward the town. Its name, Highcard, seemed grimly symbolic. This man had drawn a low card, if not the joker. It was probably too late to be of much help, but Nels brought fresh water, washing the haggard face, getting a little into the mouth. At first there was no reaction. Then the sick man coughed, choked, and swallowed thirstily.

Placing a hand behind his back, Nels raised him somewhat, giving him more to drink. As he lowered him back, the injured man's eyes opened, his head turning slightly toward the light. Nels experienced a double sense of shock.

It was nearly a decade and a half since he'd seen this man, but as he was more clearly revealed, he knew that he was not mistaken. This man was his uncle Bart Ondane.

The things he had learned, his own increasing suspicions, had been partial preparation, but only to a degree. Bart had ridden this way on business weeks before. The letter which they had received from the lawyer had reported how he had been taken ill and died, then been buried in the town of Highcard.

Something, apparently many things, were drastically wrong.

Had there been any room for doubt, that was removed as Bart's eyes widened, fixing on Nels in turn. He'd been a small boy when Bart had last seen him, but Draine had had no difficulty in recognizing Nels as an Ondane. Recognition came into the injured man's eyes, a momentary excitement which ebbed almost as swiftly.

'Nels!' he managed. The word was like a croak, and there was something of horror as well as fear in his eyes. He spoke falteringly. 'You here, boy? I've been a fool. I didn't understand—or intend—'

He tried desperately to continue, but the effort was too much. Gasping, he sank back. Nels knew that he had spoken his last words.

CHAPTER NINE

Nels discovered a rusty shovel with a broken handle half-buried among the weeds and brush near the spring. With it, he managed to dig a grave at the edge of the meadow. Once the task was completed, he pondered soberly, remembering his uncle's last request as outlined in the letter they had received: that they place a marker, some sort of headstone, above his grave.

This was the grave, but Nels shook his head. There was a mystery here, grimmer and more bloody than he liked to contemplate, and what he understood or suspected that he understood ran counter to supposedly known facts. It might be better to leave this mound of dirt without a clue as to its occupancy, at least for the present.

Bequests are one thing, he reflected. Bullets are something else. And I'd like to know where they tie in together—providing they do.

The cabin afforded no clue to the mystery, or to why Bart had ridden off this way, ostensibly on business; actually—and apparently—to die. There had been no papers on his person, nothing to suggest an answer. That, of course, was hardly surprising, for whoever had fired the bushwhack bullet might well have robbed him afterward.

He let it be known that he was heading toward Highcard on business, Nels summed the situation up in his mind. But he must have aimed to hide out here while the report went back that he was dead—which would put his will into effect and bring us out to the saloon. Things were supposed to happen then, and he'd sit back and pull the strings. Only something went wrong, instead of the way he'd planned.

As he set out again, the other cayuse wanted to come along. It required some maneuvering to lose it, and leaving the lonesome pony made him feel like a heel. But if it tagged along with him, there might be questions, perhaps doubly bad if they went unvoiced. Somebody might recognize it as being the horse that Bart Ondane had ridden.

He had no further trouble finding the town. Highcard sprawled near the foot of Baldy, the trading center for a few scattered ranches and occasional trappers or prospectors.

Finding a livery stable for his horse, Nels engaged the proprietor in conversation.

'I'm new in this part of the country,' he explained, 'looking for a man named Ondane—or his grave, I guess,' he added, and managed a lopsided grin.

The stableman had been sucking at a straw. All at once it was bitten off-short with a click of teeth.

'Ondane, you say?' he repeated carefully. 'Would that be Bart Ondane that you're meaning?'

'That was his name, near as I recollect. Seems to me he belonged in another part of the country.'

'And you say you're looking for his grave?'

Nels grinned ingenuously. It seemed unlikely that anyone in the vicinity would know the Ondanes well enough to recognize him as one.

'Well, I am and I ain't,' he explained, and went on, pleased with his flight of fancy. 'It's this way. I was down by the railroad, kind of between jobs—not lookin' too hard for a new one, you understand, but willing if a good one came along. A man approached me. Said he'd had a letter from back East, from a man who wanted to hire somebody to ride up this way and see about e-rectin' a marker over a grave. Said demised being named Ondane. There was money to pay for what was wanted, and it sounded like it wouldn't be a bad ride. So here I am.'

He grinned again, thinking how shocked August or Mary would be at such shameless prevarication. But there was at least a hard kernel of truth in the story, and the circumstances seemed to justify caution. The stableman chewed reflectively.

'I reckon you've come to the right place for

that chore,' he agreed. 'Kind of a sad case, this Ondane. Leastwise it would have been with anybody but him.'

'How do you mean?' It was no trouble to look perplexed. 'What's the difference?'

'Well, actually I suppose there ain't none, when a man dies. I guess one way leaves him just as dead as another, and where he goes from here is mostly his worry, not ours. But I reckon there's not much doubt as to *which* way Bart Ondane must have gone.'

'I sort of gather that he wasn't too popular a character around here. Or am I gettin' my trails tangled?'

'Well, around here folks didn't much care, not hardly knowing him. But back to the east a ways, around Mockery, in the Valley of the Gun—that was his country—Bart Ondane was about as popular as a double dose of the seven-year itch. You could say he was the best-hated man in a wide stretch of country. But of course he's dead, and if somebody wants to put a marker over what's left of him—why, I guess there's nothing wrong with the notion.'

'Somebody shoot him, or something?'

'Oh no, nothing like that. Not here. We're peaceful and law-abidin' in this country. If it had been his own range, now—but anyway, he came to this town a few weeks back, a mighty sick man. I happened to be standin' right here in the door of the stable, looking out, and I saw him coming. His horse was pacin' slow-like, and he was all slumped over, clutchin' at the saddle-horn to keep from falling.

'First off I didn't recognize him, but we got him down from his horse and did what we could, which wasn't much. He was a mighty sick man, just barely conscious. We never could be sure just what had hit him,' the stableman added solemnly. 'My notion, from what experience I've had that way, was that it must've been something he'd et. Poisoned him, looked like. We tried to doctor him, but there's no real medico nowhere in these parts. He up and died that same night.'

Here, Nels reflected, was prevarication to throw his own into the shade. It was a good enough story, bolstered by the grave which they showed him, and all quite in accord with the account which the lawyer had given. Bart Ondane was officially dead and buried here, with any number of witnesses who would testify accordingly. Probably all but a handful believed what they would tell.

Nels was intrigued, but he was careful not to show it. Whose was the original plot, and where had it gone wrong? Did they really suspect that Bart Ondane was actually dead? The bushwhacker, some vengeful enemy, might have taken advantage of a tailor-made opportunity, and others in the plot been none the wiser. Who or what was back of some of these developments, and was this grave as empty as he was sure that it must be?

He listened with a straight face to whatever he was told, asking a few questions which elicited no additional information, and arranged with the local blacksmith for the marker. Since the smith had some skill at carving, a small granite boulder would be chiseled with name and date and placed at the head of the grave.

When he again rode unhurriedly out of town, Nels was convinced that no one was particularly interested in him; nonetheless, he headed west, before making a turn north and then east, in case anyone should be watching. If they guessed that his destination was the Valley of the Gun, which had been Bart Ondane's stamping ground, they might wonder.

He intended to retrace the course which he had followed, seeing without being seen. It was entirely possible that, with Bart's death, trouble was at an end, his scheme or plot already withered on the vine. On the other hand, others might be watering the vine, and the thing might be coming toward an even uglier fruition.

Once over the pass, he realized that somewhere he'd missed his former route. That didn't matter, since he would work toward the middle of the valley and so on north, but this was even rougher terrain than he'd crossed before. There were range on range of mountains, with twisted canyons between. Yet once across the main pass, he had still been doing a lot of climbing, walking most of the time to aid his horse. The air was thin and sharp. Pine-clad slopes sawed at the sky.

It seemed doubtful to him this land would be owned or even claimed by any of the valley outfits. On some of these slopes the grass would afford excellent graze, but the country was ruggedly wild. Neither that day nor the preceding one had he sighted either a man or a human habitation. Except for an innate streak of stubbornness, he would have turned back, heading for the road and the longer route into the valley at the north, by Mockery. He was learning a lot, but it was impressed upon him that he was still very much a tenderfoot.

At this elevation the climate was still early spring, though summer had touched the lower valleys. Nels found himself exhilarated by it all. This was challenging country, lonely and aloof, as it must have been when the world was young.

His pony snatched a few bites of grass, reminding Nels that his pack was getting thin. He'd have to shoot some game for supper. As though the thought of a gun conjured one up, a rifle's sharp crash broke the silence. Thunder cascaded among the crags.

His pony jerked in startled apprehension. The sound was followed by another, even less pleasant—this the shrill, high keening of a dog, a wail of agony.

The tortured cry rose, then was gone as abruptly. Nels shivered in understanding. The sudden ending to such a clamor could mean only one thing: death.

CHAPTER TEN

The dog's high keening had barely subsided when it was answered by another; only this cry was human. In the sound was blended rage, pity and dismay. Most startling and unsettling of all, the voice was a woman's.

A shower had ranged through this section of hills not long before. Nels had seen the storm clouds, the sweep of rain like a moving wall, though it had missed the place where he climbed. Drops of water still sparkled on leaves and grass as the sun broke through a shrouding mist, leaving a new-washed fragrance on the air. The sounds which had assaulted his ears seemed increasingly alien and out of place.

As he kicked his horse into motion, the richness of the air was tainted by a new and alien odor drifting on the light breeze. The smell caused his nostrils to pinch with remembered distaste. One summer, along with his aunt and uncle, they had lived as neighbors to a man who ran sheep. That had been nothing new, for small bands of sheep were common on eastern farms; only in that case, there had been far too many animals for the space available. They had been kept too closely crowded, especially at night, when confined in a shed. The resultant stench, built up over a period of years, sometimes filled the valley.

Ever since, Nels had disliked the smell of sheep. It was sheep odor which came now.

He shoved recklessly through a screen of brush, instead of circling around it, and the disturbed raindrops showered on him. Then he came out at the edge of a high meadow, one of numerous mountain uplands.

His nose had not played him false. Sheep were streaming across the meadow, pushing eagerly, as though drawn by a lure toward spreading clumps of tufted flowers which sparkled like snow. The sheep were beginning to graze hungrily, finding the rain-wet provender especially to their taste. Nels estimated that there might be half a thousand in the band.

Closer at hand he saw the dog and the girl. He had an impression of lithe slenderness in Levis, as she jumped down from her horse and ran to drop on her knees where the dog lay sprawled, cradling it in her arms. A wide-brimmed hat partially concealed a mass of reddish-gold hair, confirming his first impression that the herder was a girl.

The dog, a collie, made a last feeble gesture, raising its head, red tongue flicking out, attempting to caress the face of the girl. Then it fell back, the gesture half-completed.

At the sound of the oncoming horse, the girl turned a grief-stricken face, numb with shock. Even in her disarray, she appeared pretty and graceful. She stared at him uncomprehendingly, then came suddenly to her feet. Before he realized what she intended, hot eyes were blazing at him above the blued barrel of a revolver.

Nels watched with wonder and admiration, even as he eyed the muzzle of the gun with respect. The weapon seemed huge and out of place in her hands, but it was held steadily, and the draw had been creditably fast. The face behind the gun, despite its grief and anger, was worth any man's attention.

'Stop right where you are!' she ordered, while her voice choked on a sob. 'You murdering killer! I ought to shoot you, too! Look at what you've done!'

Nels obeyed, dividing his attention between the girl and the collie, though a second glance was enough to assure him that the dog was dead. A gaping wound in the shoulder, where a soft-nosed rifle bullet had torn, was bleeding freely.

The girl's gun he took to be a forty-five, not a small caliber such as a woman might be expected to carry. Clearly, in this country she went prepared for trouble. He was mildly reassured to observe that, despite her anger, her hand was steady. Uncertainty had no place on a trigger at such a time.

Nels took pains to remain both poised and unhurried. With one hand he held the bridle reins. With his other, he reached and doffed his hat.

'Not me, miss,' he denied. 'You can take a look at my gun, if you like; I'm sure that you know enough about a weapon to tell that it hasn't been fired since it was last cleaned. In any case, I'd not shoot a dog in such a fashion.'

The girl's eyes widened, a touch of color replacing the sudden pallor of her cheeks. She studied him with sharp attention, considering his offer. It could be a trick, though; having the drop as she did, she should be able to control the situation.

With increasing surprise she saw that he was younger than she had supposed, only a year or so beyond her own age, and decided to re-assess her first impression that he was a cowboy. He had an easy manner in the saddle, and the gun-belt and holster looked right, but he wore shoes instead of boots, and those were a dead giveaway. Also, he was clean shaven, no longer ago than the day before, and that was both unusual and, in her eyes, a mark in his favor.

Her gun barrel made a small wavering gesture. Coloring with confusion, she returned the weapon to its holster.

'Oh, I'm sorry.' She was accepting his word. 'But someone just shot Hector, and I supposed—'

As her gaze ranged on toward the sheep, she broke off, only to leap up, exclaiming in fresh consternation. The stragglers in the band were still rushing forward, but the foremost animals had reached the flowering clumps and were grazing hungrily.

'They'll be poisoned! That's camas—and whoever shot my dog must have killed him just so that I wouldn't be able to control them or turn them away from it! They'll all be killed.'

She swung about, frantic with haste, not even looking back to see what his reaction might be. Reaching her horse, she jumped into the saddle with no encumbrance of skirts, then sent it racing toward the sheep, shouting in an effort to turn them. Nels suddenly understood the seriousness of the situation.

Camas! Death camas, as it was sometimes called, was sheep weed, and that explained a lot. Much of the high country of the valley was disputed territory, vied for by rival cattle and sheep outfits. It looked as though the uneasy truce had finally been shattered. These animals would be from one of the sheep ranches; apparently the girl and her dog had been driving the band to a new pasture.

It was surprising to find a woman so directly involved, but someone, undeterred by any sense of chivalry, had seen his chance and taken advantage of it. The bullet which had dropped the dog had come from ambush. Up to now, at least, the bushwhacker was keeping discreetly out of sight. Undoubtedly he figured that the combination of circumstances, the sheep weed temptingly at hand and the dog out of the way, would be enough to accomplish his purpose.

The fluffy flowers of the camas were rendered doubly tasty by the recent shower. The ground all along the far edge of the meadow was adance with the blossoms.

Lovely in appearance, luscious to the taste, the weed was highly toxic to sheep, though they lacked any instinct to warn them of its deadly nature. If left alone, they would not be long in finding out. If allowed to eat their fill, the entire band might be poisoned.

They had been following a course where, along the rim of a slope, held to the trail and hurried by the dog, they would have been ushered safely past the danger. Now, left to scatter as they pleased, it was a different story.

Nels jumped his own horse, bringing it even with the girl's, jerking loose the lariat tied beside the saddle-horn. It had been useful for picketing his horse at night, but would serve another purpose. He swung the coiled rope, slapping the heavy strands sharply against tender noses.

His horse snorted its dislike of the procedure, so that he guessed that it had spent its days among cows. Despite that, it did its part, even while baffled by the reaction of the sheep. They did not respond to such chousing as cattle would have done, but clung stubbornly to their purpose of stuffing themselves. The girl, pale with desperation, worked frantically to get them moving, handicapped by the loss of the dog.

The leaders of the band had tasted the weed and were eager for more, while those behind kept crowding, determined to get their share. They resisted efforts to swing them away with a resigned sort of stubbornness more frustrating than active opposition.

Alone, either Nels or the girl would have been helpless, since one section of the band would flow back while others were being forced away. Working together, they gradually urged the sheep into motion, then shoved them along at a quickening pace. Blatting their protest, all but a few stragglers were presently heading on down the trail. The ones which remained were already showing the effects of their feast, proof of the deadly potency of the weed.

There was nothing to be done for those who had eaten too much, but most of the band appeared to be safe. Nels dropped the coiled rope over the saddle-horn and mopped at his face. It was hot in the sun, and unreasoning anger at those who would fight in so underhand a manner, especially against a girl, made him feel worse. He even felt sympathy for the sheep, lured toward destruction in so insidious a manner.

Brushing back a loose strand of hair, the girl smiled at him.

'Thanks,' she gasped. 'They'll be all right now. That's the only patch of sheep weed anywhere around here. I couldn't have managed without your help. And to think that I accused you of shooting my dog!'

'It was a natural conclusion, under the circumstances,' Nels pointed out. 'First there was the shot; then I showed up.'

'But if I'd taken a better look at you, I should have known that you weren't that kind of person.' Color raced in her cheeks; then she changed the subject. 'I could use a drink. How about you? There's a good spring, just back from the trail here.'

As Nels agreed, she led the way, pushing her horse between tall trees to where a spring bubbled from under a massive rock formation. Allowing their horses to drink at the overflow, they slaked their own thirst, washing hands and faces.

Both looked up together from opposite sides of the little pool, meeting each other's eyes. The girl colored under his regard.

'I am awfully sorry about making such a mistake and pulling a gun on you,' she said contritely. 'I guess that was a pretty awful thing to do.'

'Don't let it worry you,' Nels returned. 'I expect that I'd have figured just about the same way, under the circumstances. What counts is saving the sheep.'

'Yes,' she agreed. 'It would have been terrible if I'd lost the whole band.' Her eyes darkened at the thought. 'I told Dad that I could manage fine. They needed to be moved, and we're short-handed, since a couple of the herders quit without warning, and Dad is not well.' Again she changed the subject. 'You're new in this country, aren't you?'

'Yes,' Nels acknowledged. 'But it's wonderful country—leaving out some of the inhabitants.'

'Not everybody is sneaky or a trouble-maker,' she defended it. 'I don't think there's any other place to match this valley, at least when it's left the way God made it.' With a touch of bitterness she added. 'Men, some men, can spoil anything.'

'It doesn't take much,' Nels agreed. 'Paradise was that way to begin with, I suppose. Nature gives us something fine to start with, after which we have to make what we consider improvements, and spoil things as fast as possible.'

She nodded agreement.

'Somebody planned to stir up real trouble by shooting my dog, then destroying the sheep. But since it didn't work, I don't think that I'll say anything about what happened. There's plenty of tension already, all through the valley, without my making it worse.'

CHAPTER ELEVEN

Their horses were moving about with dragging reins, cropping the grass. The girl found a pleasantly shaded spot and sat down, and Nels followed suit. She studied him with frank curiosity.

'Of course it's none of my business,' she observed, 'but strangers are pretty scarce in this country. You must be new hereabouts.'

'I am,' he agreed. 'If I look and act like a tenderfoot, that's because I am. Until a few days ago, I'd never been west of Buffalo.' At the puzzlement in her eyes, he explained: 'Buffalo, New York.'

'Oh.' She studied him with fresh interest.

'That's way back East! I've never been as far east as Dakota, even.'

'You live hereabouts, I suppose?'

'Yes. I'm Sue MacDonald. My folks own one of the ranches—one of the sheep outfits.'

From the way in which she said it, he gathered that the MacDonalds were of consequence in the valley.

'I'm Nels Ondane. My uncle was Bart Ondane.'

As he had anticipated, the name meant something to her, and it was not favorable. She drew a quick breath.

'Bart Ondane—your uncle? But he—he's dead.'

'Yes. That's why I'm here. My folks had a letter from a lawyer, a Mr. Crockett, telling us about it. He left some property to us.'

'Well, he had property, all right.' She pondered, as though uncertain. 'But you're alone, and a long way from Mockery.'

'We came there, but Uncle Bart died down at Highcard, so I went there to do one or two little things.'

'You mean you've been there and are going back—all alone?' The amazement in her tone suggested that, for a tenderfoot, he was doing rather well.

'Why, what's there to that?' he asked. 'Following up or down the valley, one could hardly get lost.'

'Plenty of people have,' she assured him

gravely. 'But I've heard it said that Bart Ondane could go anywhere, even at night or in a storm, and never lose his way.' As though she found the similarity disturbing, she glanced to where the sun was westering and sprang to her feet.

'It's getting late, and the sheep will be straying again unless I keep after them. I want to thank you for helping as you did. If you keep north by east, you'll come to the main road. But I suppose you know that.'

He sensed that his being an Ondane had shocked her; against that, she was weighing what he had done, also that he had been raised thousands of miles away. Even so, he was hardly welcome there.

She caught her horse and swung into the saddle, then turned back, as though having second thoughts.

'You will be welcome at our place. But as you can see, there's trouble in this valley, so watch your step! Goodbye.'

She was gone then, riding fast after the vanishing sheep, far along the trail. Nels shook his head, tempted to follow and offer help in getting them to their destination, but decided against it. Clearly, Ondane was a name which engendered distrust, to say the least. Sue MacDonald was capable, though she had been caught off-guard by the shooting of the dog. She knew where she was going and what she was doing, and quite clearly she didn't want him tagging along.

Remembering the shot which had killed the dog, the unknown bushwhacker, he found a vantage-point and watched while the sheep descended, until they were finally lost to view and night came down. He moved back from the trail they had followed before camping. And after his cook-fire was out, he moved again, another half-mile, as silently as could be managed. This seemed to be a country for hidden bullets.

But there was no further sign of the gunman. It was afternoon again when the unbroken silence made him suspicious. He had come to sense two kinds of silence in this high country. One was the normal peace of an untroubled day, when birds sang and small creatures scurried. He'd known similar life in Eastern woodlands. The normal noises, muted and distinct, had been all about as he rode. Now, all at once, they were hushed.

In the new quality of silence he caught the ripple of a creek along a stony course, the sigh of wind in the tree-tops—those and nothing more. Nearer at hand, nature seemed to hold its breath, and in that was not only warning but a suggestion of fear.

The trail had been descending, with occasional grassy meadows, which ended now and again against sheer cliffs that fell away to dizzy space. Here was another meadow, and the hush was explained, even as it was broken.

Sheep grazed, a closely bunched band of perhaps a thousand head. They made a gray-white splash against the green background, curiously dotted or freckled with crimson. Those were blotches of red paint, used in lieu of brands, one spot to a sheep, applied near the right ear. Seen as a whole, the dobs of paint gave the impression of smallpox pitting a vast disordered body.

The sheep were grazing, undisturbed. But closer at hand, stark against the drop-off of a high ledge, were human actors, and this was the threat which had brought the hush of fear to this bit of the high cuntry. There were four men, and three of them menaced the other one. The trio were armed, while the stripling whom they menaced just as clearly was not.

The boy gave the appearance of having outgrown his clothes in a sudden rush to become a man. He was tall and thin, pants-legs and shirt-sleeves revealing overlong expanses of ankles and wrists. A saddled horse grazed near the sheep, and the sun caught a strip of rifle-barrel where it was thrust into a saddle-sheath. Clearly, the herder had been surprised, well away from horse or gun.

A copious crop of freckles stood out against the sudden paleness of his skin, while he warily watched the men who hemmed him in on three sides. The open cliff was behind him, only a few steps away. The cowboys were closing in on him, advancing slowly but relentlessly, as deadly as the closing of a wolf pack.

The man in the middle was clearly the leader, a twisted smile turning his face malignant. This was Draine of the Axe—Draine, whom August had thrown out of the saloon, and whose son Lance had tried to make Nels take a drink the next day.

They had dismounted, leaving their own horses. Each carried a gun at the ready. The studied carelessness with which they toyed with the weapons served to enhance the threat.

Not many horses in the farming country of New York and Pennsylvania wore brands, but Nels had learned to study them when they were to be found. He read those on the four horses, finding a surprising variety. A dun-colored cayuse sported a broad axe head on its left flank, and he guessed that to be Draine's. A black pony carried the whitish scar of a burned ox-bow on its right ribs, partially hidden by the saddle. The other horse of the trio was branded K-T, on the right shoulder.

He could not make out the brand on the herder's mount, but it did not match any of the others.

The dismounted men seemed more wolf-like than while in the saddle. All three were curiously of a height and size, but two were dark, while Draine, like his son, was fair.

Such odds, three against one, armed men against a defenseless boy, would have been bad enough in any case. But a still more sinister aspect was the drop-off just behind the herder, and the manner in which they advanced, forcing him back. There was more than enough depth to assure a broken mass of flesh and bone at the bottom.

The unhidden eagerness in the faces of his tormentors showed that such was their intent, to crowd him to a final backward step. The game they played might have been a grimmer extension of that upon which Nels had come the day before.

In both cases, it was clearly cattlemen against the sheep. Once the herder was out of the way, the sheep would be lost.

Up to then, there had been no spoken word, nothing to mitigate the deadly quality of the silence. Now Draine spoke.

'Might's well make it easy for yourself, Bub.' His tone was a purr. 'Just step back. Be as easy as fallin' off a log. Or would you rather have us fill you full of lead?'

The boy swallowed with a painful gulp before he could speak. When he did manage, the words were defiant.

'Go ahead and shoot,' he challenged. 'That's what you don't want—is for me to be found with bullet holes in me! Well, blast you, you'll have to put them there!'

The trio checked their slow advance, eying each other questioningly. Apparently they had overlooked that angle, or had supposed that he would, when they made the threat. One glanced toward where the sheep grazed, undisturbed, unaware of impending disaster.

'He's right, Draine. We don't want bullet holes, nothin' that'll show, not at this stage of the game.'

'I don't know that it matters too much, when it comes to that.' Draine shrugged. 'But there's other ways, Hennessey.'

'Yeah?'

'Sure. We could use the sheep. Stampede them right at him, then on over the cliff.'

The third man shook his head in prompt dissent. 'Killing that many sheep for nothing would be a big waste.'

'What's that to you, Marsh?' Draine argued. 'They're sheep, ain't they? And there'll have to be a lot of that before we're finished, to make it clear that we mean business. Anyway, we ain't footing the bill.'

Marsh remained stubborn, his eyes greedy as they studied the sheep. 'They can be sold for a lot of money. Maybe some of it'll have to be done, but not now.'

Hennessey shrugged, taking another step forward, spreading the fingers of his open hand suggestively. 'There's plenty of other ways, if you don't want to use bullets,' he pointed out.

Marsh, for all his boldness, appeared reluctant actually to compass murder. He spoke tentatively.

'The kid's scared. Maybe, if we'd give him a chance, he'd see the light and throw in with us.'

'Like fun!' the kid returned promptly, and his voice, despite a thread of fear, held derision and a taunt.

'We're wastin' time,' Draine cut in impatiently. 'I'll handle this.'

Nels, unnoticed, had watched and listened. Engrossed in the matter at hand, they clearly had no inkling that anyone else might be around.

He found himself shivering in sympathy with the kid. It would be risky to be a witness to these proceedings, to say nothing of trying to interfere. Also, leaving out immediate consequences, there was the danger of getting involved, of serious trouble later on, which might concern his folks.

But, scared as he was, Nels knew that he couldn't stand by and watch a helpless fellow-being destroyed in such a fashion. For the moment he had forgotten his own gun. In any case, it might prove to be a handicap rather than a help; it would be risky to attempt his own moderate dexterity with a six-gun against the skill of a trio of experts.

Suiting action to his words, Draine started toward the kid. Nels' voice sounded strange in his own ears.

'Hold it!' he warned, and all three jerked about at the command. Surprise held them temporarily motionless, and he went on with a steadiness which the twisting inside him belied: 'Let's talk this over.'

They had embarked upon a desperate game, a variation of the ancient feud between sheepmen and cattlemen. Whatever degree of tolerance or even of amity might have prevailed between the opposing factions in years past, the death of Bart Ondane had changed that. Now they were moving to bring about a showdown, deliberately forcing the issue. And for that, Nels realized with a sudden coldness, two victims would be better than one.

The three watched, uncertainly at first, then with growing contempt. Recognition flared in Draine's eyes, and with it was wild rage, countered by the same uncertainty which had come to him the other evening in the street. He had turned away from a fight then, but the poor quality of the light and lively superstition had played a part. Looking upon an Ondane, he had had the wild notion that a dead man was confronting him.

Now he knew better; moreover, this was the man who had also succeeded in humiliating his son.

Hope flared for an instant in the herder's face, then faded as he read the signs. Here was a brash interloper, confronting a deadly trio empty-handed. It seemed that the least which he might have done would be to get the drop on them before speaking.

Draine checked his stride. Then, understanding, he expressed his feelings by holstering his own gun.

'What's there to talk about?' he demanded. 'Would it be the price of tea in New York, now? And is this any of your business, Ondane?'

'Seems like it might be,' Nels returned, and his nervousness was gone. 'There must be better ways to settle matters than by a killing, where it wouldn't count for much in any case.'

Marsh nodded thoughtfully, but Hennessey's face was congested.

'I don't know but what he's got a point there. Maybe this needs to be made stronger—doubled, as it were! That your notion, Draine?'

Marsh temporized. He was aware of a disconcerting factor here. Not only was an Ondane intervening, but he was daring to involve himself in such fashion while keeping his gun holstered.

'Reckon we can be reasonable about this, eh?' he asked uncertainly. 'Why don't we give him a chance—to turn around and ride out, and forget he saw anything?'

'That's about what I'd expect from a weasly turncoat that smells of sheep!' Hennessey's fury was explosive. 'The devil with you—and with him!' He moved to the attack, big hands opening for the shove.

Nels had made use of the interval to move closer. The only chance, for either the herder or himself, lay in doing the unexpected. A touch of spurs sent his horse forward in a rush, overtaking Hennessey. Nels allowed the knotted ends of the reins to drop over the saddle-horn, leaving his hands free.

Hennessey was almost upon his victim when a hand closed on his coat collar, another fastening on an arm just below his shoulder. He was hefty, but less so than a couple of sacks of potatoes, and he was lifted and suspended suddenly over the brink of the ledge, while Nels' horse stopped of its own accord. Unnerved by the sight of dizzy space beneath, Hennessey did not even struggle.

The heavy chores of a farm had toughened Nels, and the stimulus of the moment made him reckless. Hennessey's courage, which had been tested and proven in numerous frays, ebbed as he gazed slack-jawed at the feathery tops of evergreens far below. His dismay was matched by the surprise of his companions. They had guns, but all at once those were not the answer.

'Drop your guns,' Nels snapped. 'Or else

I'll drop *him*!'

Draine and Marsh weighed the alternatives for only a moment. Hennessey had been the leader in this venture to begin with, and Marsh had gone along, but without much enthusiasm. Draine, despite himself, was hampered by an almost superstitious fear of this Ondane, so recklessly like the other in some respects.

Worse, Hennessey's peril was real. Should they attempt counteraction, a bullet could kill Nels, but by that very act they would assure Hennessey's destruction. Marsh's face held a greenish tint, in contrast to the mixed emotions of Draine. After a moment they obeyed. Nels nodded to the herder.

'Get their guns,' he advised, then released his captive, as his horse, as if sensing what was required, backed a couple of steps. Hennessey hit the ground and sprawled like a doll from which the sawdust had spilled, then scrambled back from the brink on hands and knees. His face, ruddy a moment before, had the look of drying clay.

Nels' gun was untouched in its holster, but the others yielded their weapons against the double threat. Hennessey, conscious of the ludicrous figure he cut, hesitated, but followed suit.

'You win this time,' he grated, getting to his feet. 'But you stick around this country, and there'll be another time! Better do as

Marsh suggested an' ride out—though I'm hopin' you ain't got that much good sense!'

Nels surveyed him carefully before replying. That was probably as sound a piece of advice as he would ever receive, but he knew that he wouldn't take it.

'I guess I never did have good sense that way,' he acknowledged. 'When it comes to riding, I'd say that it's you fellows who had better get going. If you linger, I might be tempted to put you afoot.'

CHAPTER TWELVE

Nothing more was said as the trio mounted their horses and rode from sight, spurring as they reached a gap in the trees at the far rim of the meadow. However much chastened and temporarily dehorned, they were sullen and dangerous. It occurred to Nels once again that he'd had the luck commonly associated with fools and tenderfeet, especially at the last. It was certainly sheer luck that none of the three had had a saddle-gun, a possibility he had forgotten about.

Not until they were out of sight did the herder ease a sighing breath and turn, his face puckered with mingled soberness and elation.

'Gee, Man, but that was something, the way you handled Hennessey,' he breathed.

'And him counted as just about the toughest hombre in the whole valley, not to mention Draine! I'm right grateful to you. But you've made some bad enemies.'

'Looks like both of us have, but at least we're alive,' Nels pointed out. 'They seemed to have it in for you. Was there some particular reason for such hostility?'

The herder frowned, scuffing the dirt with the toe of one heavy boot. Clearly he was troubled by the same question.

'Nothing that I know of,' he confessed. 'The whole thing's got me guessing. Their turning hostile all at once, I mean. Of course, there's been bad blood, more or less, between sheepmen and cattlemen, but seems like this was different. Like Marsh, there. He's been a herder, workin' for Orey Zumwalt, and seems like he's gone over to the other side. He showed up, alone, and seemed friendly, so when the others sneaked up sudden, they caught me plumb off guard. Draine boasted that they were going to clean every sheep and sheepman out of the valley, starting with me. And I don't think they were bluffing.'

'No, it didn't look that way. Just who is this Hennessey?'

'I could give you two answers there. The part that's known is that he's foreman for Ox-Bow. That was Bart Ondane's outfit, so he's running it now that Ondane's gone. Acts like he figures it's his now, and that he can take over the whole country. He's just mean and crazy enough to try it, too. Ox-Bow borders Axe on the North, and him and Draine pal around together.'

'What's the other answer?'

'Mostly guesswork, but I've heard that he had a different name when he came to this part of the country, but left it behind. You can sort of see what that means.'

'What you say adds up. But they really seemed to have it in for you.'

'Sort of, though I don't figure it was personal. I don't count for that much. I guess I just happened to be handy, along with the sheep, and so furnished an excuse they could use to stir up a ruckus.'

He hesitated, plainly curious, but too polite to probe deeply. Tentatively he gave his name.

'I'm Floyd Clayton. And I sure appreciate the way you helped me out. I figured I was a goner till you showed up.'

'My friends call me Nels,' Nels returned. 'You heard them call me Ondane. I'm from the East, but Bart Ondane was my uncle.'

A strained look replaced the grin on Floyd's face. It was as though he had sought to discredit the evidence of his ears, but could do so no longer. Ondane, even the name, made most people uneasy.

'Uncle, eh? Well, he was quite a fellow in these parts. Uh—these sheep belong to Old

MacDonald, and from the looks of the sun, I'd better be getting them down off this hill and back to the corrals without no more foolin'.'

So these were MacDonald sheep also. Were they being especially picked on, or was that merely coincidence? If this was MacDonald graze, then Sue had been a long way from home the day before. His ignorance of the local situation was a handicap.

Nels cast an eye to where the long shadows reached far down the mountain. 'That might be a good idea,' he concurred. 'Need any help?'

'Thanks, but I guess I can manage all right. I've got a dog around here some place—now where the dickens is that mutt, anyhow? He's usually on the job.'

He whistled, a loud, clear note, but it brought no response. Nels, remembering the fate of Sue MacDonald's dog, was not too surprised. Floyd whistled again, then began questing about anxiously. Nels helped him look, and presently they came upon the dog at the edge of the trees, concealed in a patch of brush and high grass. Struggling futilely, it was trussed and gagged by several lengths of rope.

Nels was surprised that the trio, having in mind so vicious an action, had only roped and tied the dog instead of killing it outright. Apparently they had wanted to surprise

Clayton, and to shoot it would have given warning. No doubt they had intended to release the dog and reclaim the rope, after dealing with him.

The dog whined eagerly when released. It took a few stumbling steps, then went racing off to round up the sheep and start them moving, toward a trail faintly visible at the rim of the slope.

'I'm sure glad he's all right,' Floyd exclaimed. 'I couldn't manage without him. He knows this business better than any man. If they'd killed him—'

It was clear that he had no thought of quitting his job, despite his harrowing experience, or what the future might be expected to hold.

That was probably a sound philosophy. Running away from a problem never really solved it. Nels had discovered that during the endless years when August had moved from one run-down farm to another, always hoping that the new would be better, impatient and unable to stay and fight the problems which were always present in one form or another. August called it taking advantage of new opportunities; Nels had come to realize that it was a form of quitting, of running away.

He walked with Floyd, both leading their horses, gradually working lower, with the sheep streaming ahead. With a dog to do the work, it was easy. Floyd, his first fears of an

Ondane dissipated, discussed the situation.

'Like you may know, there's seven sheep ranches and seven cattle outfits in and around this valley, all of them good-sized spreads. The sheepmen have had one big advantage. They were here first, so they had their pick. They own the heart of the valley, and all their lands are connected. That gives them strength, makes them hard to hit. But the cattlemen are along the rims, and they surround and flank the sheep. So now they're startin' to put the squeeze on us.'

Nels was puzzled. 'In that case, aren't you off your base, up so high in the hills? And I saw some other sheep way high in the mountains. If you trespass, it must naturally rile the cattlemen.'

'I guess you've got a point there, but boundaries are loose and sometimes poorly defined. Sure it makes for trouble, but it works both ways. For instance, just a little while back, Van Sickle pushed a big herd of his Boxed B stock down on MacDonald's land, and cleaned off half of his winter graze before they were discovered. So you can't blame MacDonald for swiping some back in turn.'

'Well, with things the way they are, better not stray too far from your gun next time.'

'I sure won't aim to again,' he agreed fervently. 'That was mighty scary, and if you hadn't happened along like you did—'

He swallowed, closing his eyes, then forcing a smile. He was older than Nels had first thought, the impression of youth due in part to the outgrown garments. Gangling and awkward, the kid was slow in maturing, but he had qualities of loyalty and perseverance such as the job required.

They topped another rise, and ahead Nels glimpsed a log barn and a cabin, then the high tiers of a sheep corral, with a huge flat roof made of poles. Here again was the pervading smell of sheep, though not so strong as to be disagreeable.

This would not be home ranch; merely an outlying station. Floyd's invitation was confirmation.

'How about havin' supper with me and spendin' the night? I'm not what you'd call a fancy cook, but I can dish up grub that'll stick to your ribs—'

There was a sudden interruption. The sheep were streaming toward the corral, where the gate stood wide. Full-fed from their day of grazing on the rich grasses of the mountain, they were eager for the security of the roofed corral. Young lambs still romped and frolicked, while their mothers tried vainly to keep a protective eye on them, complaining with plaintive resignation when that proved impossible.

A shadowy figure emerged from the doorway to the corral, moving into the open as the first sheep started to crowd through. The creature was huge, and despite an impression of clumsiness, it moved swiftly. A lamb bleated in terror. The shove of the herd, pushing from behind, threatened to hem in the intruder. It reared erect on hind legs, and now it was holding the lamb.

Nels heard the bleat, its anguish shared by the despairing mother. As usual when confronted by a new situation, Nels took time to assess it, but the herder did not. He rushed forward, leaving his horse, driven by a sort of blind desperation to attempt a rescue. Shadowed as the intruder was by the gate-posts, Nels was not sure if Floyd even understood who or what it was.

Nels had a good view. It was a bear, its brown coat shaggy, clutching its victim with its fore paws and glaring about with half-opened mouth. Most bears subsisted largely on a vegetarian and perhaps fish diet, interspersed with bugs, beetles and small rodents. Now and again, however, one would acquire a taste for flesh, of sheep, pig or cow. When that happened, they almost invariably turned into voracious killers.

Apparently the bear had drifted down to visit the empty corral, then had lurked, intending to snatch a sheep with as little fuss as possible, after which it would withdraw to feast. The sudden onrush of the homecoming band had surprised it, hemming it in, and

Floyd was adding to its sense of entrapment. He plunged ahead, circling the band as far as he could, then plunging among them. As the lamb blatted again, he jerked one of the revolvers which he had so recently acquired, emptying it at the bear at point-blank range.

It happened so swiftly that Nels had no chance to offer a word of caution, or even to reach Floyd's horse, where his rifle still reposed in its sheath. Apparently Floyd had forgotten all about the heavier gun, or else he had a blind faith in the power of a forty-five. Nels remembered the one and doubted the other, but by now the sheep were crowding between him and the rifle, so that to reach it would take too long.

Something had to be done, fast. The situation had been sharply aggravated by the sting of the bullets, which had scored hits, but apparently with no particular effect. What there was seemed merely to infuriate the bear. A brown bear somewhat resembled a grizzly in looks, and it could almost match the silvertip for viciousness. In addition, this one was big.

Nels had his own revolver, but at such a juncture he did not put much trust in a six-gun. It might kill, at close range, but he'd seen bears back in York State. When aroused, they were slow to give up, hard to kill.

Another weapon might prove better in such an emergency. The day before, he'd used the lariat to slap at the noses of the sheep, and it had been effective. Now he jerked it loose, then sent the loop shaking out in a quick cast above the milling herd.

This was chancy business, as no one knew better than he. Boyishly eager to emulate his uncle, after Bart's visit East he had spent a lot of time with a rope. Posts offered good targets, and old Shep had been both patient and long-suffering. Attaining a fair proficiency, he'd tried cows, first making the catch but unable to snub his rope, and being dragged for his pains.

If he missed the target now, there would be no time for a second try. Floyd would be mauled, or worse.

It was an advantage to be riding a well-trained pony. His horse was clearly disapproving, mistrusting the sheep and terrified of the bear, but it responded, moving automatically as the loop settled over the bear's head. The pony reared back as it jerked tight, and Nels snubbed his end of the rope around the saddle-horn.

A growl of rage started to blare up from the intruder's throat, choked suddenly to a wheeze as the noose tightened. For a moment the bear stood its ground, striking and clawing at the tormenting cord, enraged as that had no effect. Changing tactics, it began a rush, and all at once there was a melee such as nightmares are made of.

Clayton, trying desperately to get out of the way, slipped and went down, but the bear had no time for him. It lunged toward the new source of trouble, snarling and clawing, releasing its captive as of no account. Blatting in terror, the sheep tried to get out of the way, succeeding only in hampering everyone.

The pony was doing its best, trying to back and keep the rope taut. It was game, but sheep were under its feet, lunging blindly at its legs, spoiling any foothold. The bear, choking and hampered, came on. The cayuse slipped on a fallen sheep and went down. Nels, jumping to avoid being caught, found the suddenly unrestricted beast heading for him.

His feet were scooped from under him, and he found himself riding a sheep. It was going away, then shifted course abruptly, scooting blindly, straight toward the bear. A third time it shifted course, spilling Nels into the dirt, and now the bear was above him.

CHAPTER THIRTEEN

Right now his gun would be handy, but the trouble was that he couldn't get hold of it. The bear was on top of him, but Nels squirmed desperately to one side as it seemed to settle, aware of a sudden hush following the wild commotion. The bear was dead, and the frightened sheep had fled, some to huddle in the farthest reaches of the corral, others outside.

Floyd was there, a reddened knife in his hand. Whether or not it had made much difference at the last, he had closed and used it, and the bullets had finally taken effect.

'You all right?' he gasped.

'Sure. I just came along for the show,' Nels managed with sudden relief. 'But next time, man, remember your rifle. You get in too much of a rush.'

'I guess I do,' Floyd admitted ruefully, and staggered. Nels caught him, suddenly aware that Floyd had not come off unhurt. A glancing swipe of the bear's paw had furrowed his right arm from shoulder to elbow, the claws raking through shirt and skin. Blood made it look even worse.

Though sick and dizzy, he was insistent that the sheep be looked after before he would submit to going to the cabin and having his arm cared for. The dog soon accomplished the first, and Nels shut the gate on them. Building a fire in the stove, he heated water and washed the arm, then dabbed the gashes with iodine. Floyd flinched and set his teeth, but endured the pain without protest.

'If you don't mind,' he said shakily. 'I think I'll let you fix supper. Maybe it'll taste better.'

Both were more bothered by the ordeal than they liked to admit. Reaction left Nels almost as weak and shaky as the kid, but it had passed by the time he'd cooked and they had eaten a meal.

'Reckon we'd better skin the bear,' Floyd suggested, and unearthed a skinning knife of impressive proportions. 'It's sharp,' he added. 'Too bad it wasn't handy when we needed it.'

He was game, but when he almost collapsed onto the point of the knife, Nels took it from him and did most of the skinning. Peeling the pelt off was more of a chore than either had anticipated. By the time it was off, Nels was too tired to nail it to the side of the cabin.

'Just fold it together and leave it until morning,' Floyd advised. 'That'll do just as well. Me for the hay.'

He was asleep as soon as he crawled into his bunk, but that did not last long. Presently, bothered by a smarting arm, he was restless and wakeful. Nels arose a couple of times to bring him a drink, then awoke a third time at his companion's tossing. He lay a moment, drugged by sleep, then was alert, sniffing suspiciously. As he came out of the bunk, a red eye seemed to wink from the outer darkness.

Jerking open the door, Nels grabbed for

the water bucket. Flames were gnawing at a corner of the cabin, starting to spread. He sloshed the water on the fire, and the flames hesitated, hissing and steaming, then revived. It was clear that someone had slipped up under cover of darkness and set fire to the building, and no more than a guess was needed as to who might have done so. Some or all of the trio, smarting with humiliation, had returned for a cheap revenge.

A half-moon cruised the skies, giving an uncertain light. More water would be needed to smother the flames before they got beyond control. The creek where Floyd got his water, a tumbling mountain torrent, was a hundred feet away. Nels started for it at a run, clutching the empty bucket. He had taken only a dozen strides when a gun slammed from a deeper pocket of blackness, and lead whistled unpleasantly close. A second bullet tore through the tin pail, puncturing both sides, giving it a savage jerk.

Nels dropped flat, breathing hard, more scared than he liked to think about. The arsonist had holed up off there, on guard against any water being obtained to fight the flames. To keep on, exposed under the moon, would amount to suicide. To crouch and wait meant that the cabin would be destroyed.

Crouching low, Nels retreated. Reaching the shadows of the cabin opposite the fire, he ducked inside. Floyd was struggling from his bunk, dazed with sleep and bewilderment.

'What's going on?' he demanded. The restless movement of the sheep, an uneasy bleating, sounded from the corral.

'Stay inside,' Nels answered sharply. 'That crazy gunman might get a hit next time.'

He grabbed the folded bearskin, tugging so that it unfolded as he reached the doorway. The pelt was a massive trophy, and might have made a nice coat or rug, but it would serve another purpose now, or so he hoped. Mindful of the bushwhacker, he flung the wet side of the skin onto the flames, tugging and spreading it to cover where a tongue of fire still showed. A nerve-stretching awareness that more bullets might come questing at any moment hurried him.

With the big pelt smothering the flames, their light was snuffed out. The gunman was perhaps too far off to tell what was going on.

Again the gun cracked; then the sniper was outlined, coming at a run, angrily determined to finish what he had begun. He checked in midstride, lifting the gun. Nels, frantic with haste, jerked at his own weapon, lifting and triggering, scarcely taking time to aim, with the certainty that the other bullets were intended to kill.

Again the lead smashed close, thudding into the logs of the cabin, tearing loose a splinter. Then, as Nels watched incredulously, the running man wavered, pitched and lay sprawled.

Floyd was in the doorway, clutching a revolver. His voice had a mixture of awe and uncertainty.

'Looks like you got him. You'll be getting a rep in these parts!'

'That's the last thing I want,' Nels protested, then amended soberly, 'or the next to the last. I sure didn't want to shoot anybody; only he didn't give me much choice.'

Wary that this might be a trick, they advanced, but there was no further sound or movement. The fallen man lay on his face in the grass, with blood making a spreading stain. When they turned him to the light, it was Hennessey.

'You drilled him clean!' Floyd observed, and awe was strong in his voice. 'Next to Bart Ondane, he was the toughest and worst-hated man in this whole valley.' Almost in a whisper, he added: 'And you're an Ondane!'

Nels was listening for other sounds, but there was no indication that Hennessey's companions had accompanied him. Apparently this foray to burn the cabin, then shoot them as they attempted to flee, outlined against the flames, had been his own idea.

The fire was out, with the charred and ruined bearskin as a trophy. Nels lay wakeful, sure that he could not sleep after what had happened. Then he awoke to sunshine in his face, and the sounds of Floyd preparing breakfast.

There had been no further alarms during the night, proof that Hennessey had tried this on his own, spurred by humiliation as well as rage.

'Looks to me like the best way's for us to bury him and not say anything,' Floyd suggested. 'No need to go out of our way and ask for more trouble.'

Nels agreed, but he was sober once the sod had been replaced over the grave.

'There'll be questions, when he fails to show up again,' he pointed out. 'And the cattlemen will figure that they have to follow it up.'

'Likely enough,' Floyd conceded. 'Not that there'll be many tears shed on his account. But that won't make much difference.'

'Will you be taking the sheep back to your main ranch now?'

Floyd looked surprised. 'Why, no. This is where they belong. And anyway, I figure one place is about as good as another.'

* * *

Change had come to Mockery, in the interval of Nels' absence. As always at the start of any new venture, August was bubbling with enthusiasm, bustling with energy. The stock of liquor had been removed from the saloon and shifted to its new location at Mike's place. Inside, the building had received a thorough scrubbing, mostly by Mary, so that only a faint odor of its former contents clung like a taint to the woodwork or assailed the nostrils.

August had climbed on a ladder and painted out the words: 'Powdersmoke Saloon.' In their place he had lettered a new sign, for all to read: 'The Big Store. Hardware and Implements.'

Mike Harris had found the cash to pay for what he'd bought, and with that money, taking Nels' consent for granted, August had sent out an order, already in the process of being filled. Supplies appropriate to the altered nature of the store were beginning to arrive, in heavily loaded wagons. There were some tools and machinery, as well as nails and bolts, harness and saddles, guns and ammunition.

It seemed apparent to Nels, inspecting the new set-up, that August had put in a general order, leaving the items to the judgment of the supplier. That seemed to have worked out rather well, and the die was cast. They were in business, and August was confident that everyone in the valley would welcome the store.

'It's bound to fill a real need,' he pointed out. 'And this is something that we can take pride in. Make money, too.'

His mind full of the new venture, August asked few questions concerning Nels' mission and how it had gone. The fact that he had returned, roughly on schedule, and his report that he had seen the grave and arranged for the marker seemed to take care of that. Nels made no mention of the other aspects of his journey, or of finding Bart Ondane alive.

He was still doing a lot of thinking as he put his shoulder to the job of unloading the new stuff and arranging goods on shelves or against the walls. So far there had been no talk about Hennessey, no questions, but those, like some of his own, must be causing a lot of speculation. Nels straightened, mopping a sleeve across his face, as the lawyer came in, halting for a smile and a friendly word.

'You're really making a change around here,' Crockett commented. 'Just what this country's been needing, too. You folks should do well with a hardware store.'

'Maybe.' Nels studied him, then spoke deliberately. 'I've been expecting a call, for us to come to your office.'

'You have? My office?' Crockett kept his voice hearty. Dropping in for this call had been in the nature of a test. He'd been hearing things, part speculation and rumor, but with a foundation in fact, concerning this man. It was just as well to discover, if he could, how much Nels knew or suspected.

'I don't understand,' Crockett added. 'I thought our business was all taken care of.'

Blast him! he thought apprehensively. *He's like his uncle, hard to fool*. There had been no trouble with August, and if any suspicions should crop up, Crockett was certain that he could deal with them. But that episode of the Van Sickles and Larch Draine had left him uneasy. They had bungled badly, and sympathy had shifted in the community. Then, during Nels' absence, he had come to hope that matters might work out.

That had been too optimistic a philosophy, he realized now, particularly in view of the report of how this Ondane had dealt with Hennessey, and the mysterious disappearance of Hennessey thereafter.

Nels eyed him levelly. 'There are some questions that will need to be answered,' he said, 'regarding this saloon. You say it was left to us by Bart Ondane?'

August had been busy in another part of the room. Now he intervened angrily.

'I wish you wouldn't use that word, Nels. It's not a saloon—not any more.'

'It was,' Nels pointed out. 'That was Uncle Bart's idea, as I understand it.'

'Of course it was, and he left it to you folks,' Crockett agreed. 'What's there about that which you don't understand?'

'Quite a few things. Why was the saloon left to us particularly, in just such a manner?

And what about his ranch, the Ox-Bow? You haven't said a word about it—but he's dead and buried, and we're his only heirs. So it strikes me that the Ox-Bow, and maybe a lot of other property, belongs to us.'

Crockett mopped his face with a white handkerchief. He noted that August had stopped working and was listening, a startled look on his face. This was what he'd been fearing, and Nels, like Bart Ondane, hadn't overlooked it. His silence for long was the more ominous, proof that he'd been looking around, asking questions, drawing his own conclusions.

'Matters like that take time,' Crockett explained. 'The saloon was a simple matter, since he'd made particular provision concerning it in his will.' He searched desperately for a convincing answer. It would have been better never to have sent that letter East, as things had subsequently turned out, but at the time he hadn't been gifted with foresight. And of course there would have been risks involved, though certainly they were no greater than present ones. But that was water over the dam.

He'd planned, if the matter of the Ox-Bow came up at all, to bluster and deny it. But, face to face with Nels, he found it was almost as bad as when he'd faced Bart; both were Ondanes, and not easy to bluff. Also, a flat denial would probably be a mistake.

'As for the ranch—well—that's rather different,' he went on. 'The law has to be convinced that he's really dead before there can be any action taken in regard to it.'

'Before it can be turned over to us legally?' Nels probed. 'But you wrote us, weeks ago, that he was dead and buried. I can confirm that, since I traveled to Highcard and had a marker placed over his grave.'

Crockett longed to mop his face again, but the gesture would betray his uneasiness. Had Nels discovered anything on that journey? It seemed impossible—but the grave itself was suddenly a damning bit of evidence.

'Well, that's so, of course. I wrote you according to the instructions in the will. But things like this take longer—'

Anger had been building in Nels for a long while—ever since he'd come upon Bart Ondane, clinging to life, dying slowly, painfully, over a period of weeks. Perhaps his conduct, even his own scheming, had merited such an end, but that was no justification. And Crockett was involved in this, just how deeply, he intended to discover.

'You're a poor liar, Crockett,' Nels said contemptuously, 'as well as being a cheap crook. I don't know just what sort of a game you're trying to work, though I have a pretty good idea. You'd better get it through your head that it won't work. We want a full and complete settlement, without any more stalling. See to it.'

Crockett stared after him as Nels turned his back, swallowing a couple of times. Only one other man had ever dared talk to him in such fashion and been able to get away with it. And even he hadn't—in the final accounting.

He had a mind to shout after Nels, to resent the insult, but the words stuck in his throat. Crockett turned abruptly, hurrying out and back to his office. He'd been clever enough to deal with Bart Ondane, and he could certainly manage this brash young cub. The rub was the public manner in which Nels had voiced his opinions, turning them into charges, with several people about to hear. He was calling for a showdown, and he'd sure enough get it.

CHAPTER FOURTEEN

August, busy with the arrangement of goods along a shelf, had overheard, listening first with dismay that Nels would so brashly confront an attorney, then with surprise which gave way to excitement and a certain humiliation. The perfectly obvious facts which Nels had hurled at the lawyer had never occurred to him, but the manifest uneasiness of Crockett, as well as his failure to refute the charges, seemed proof that Nels had called the turn.

'I guess I've been too busy getting things changed around, too excited by this much of an inheritance, to think of anything more,' he confessed to Nels. 'You say that Bart owned a ranch, along with this?'

'One of the biggest in this part of the country,' Nels confirmed. He did not add what now seemed obvious: that Bart had been scheming to acquire a lot more of the valley, and that the first step had been to set neighbor against neighbor, creating a range war, a bloody chaos out of which he would stand ready to pick up the pieces.

'Then, if he had a ranch, you must be right. It should come to us, too.'

'It has to,' Nels said flatly. 'I've waited for Crockett to bring the matter up, but from the way he acted, it's clear enough that he didn't intend to unless his hand was forced. It looks to me as though he tried to double-cross Uncle Bart—his wishes, that is—and has been trying to do the same to us.'

'Oh, now, boy, those are pretty sweeping charges—'

'He didn't deny them,' Nels pointed out dryly.

'He offered to discuss them,' August protested, suddenly fearful that they might be going too far. 'He's been very cooperative, as we must remember. Why, he was the one who suggested that what this country stood most in need of was a hardware store.'

'Which, as a suggestion, may not be nearly so disinterested as it may have sounded,' Nels grunted, but did not explain his sudden foreboding. In this country, August was a babe in the woods, even if he had thrown Draine out of his place and gotten away with it.

August did not pursue the remark, which he found puzzling. The new suggestion regarding the ranch excited him, and he'd protested almost as a matter of habit. He regarded Nels with increased respect. He had overheard enough talk in the past day or so to realize that the name of Ondane, at least of Bart Ondane, had been one to conjure with in this valley. And something of the same prestige seemed to have attached itself to Nels.

On the street, Nels encountered Janie Harris. He stopped, pleased, as she hailed him. There was a quizzical look in her eyes.

'What's all this that I've been hearing about you, Nels?' she asked.

He laughed. 'How would I know? I've been away.'

'That's what I mean. Apparently the Ondane mantle has fallen on shoulders broad enough to wear it.'

He had never been much of a hand at dissembling, and now he did not try. Janie was too direct herself, and he owed a lot to her.

'I hope you're right about that,' he said.

'So do I.' Her eyes were sober. 'Do you realize what you folks have gotten into? I'm sure your uncle doesn't.'

'What?' he asked, though he had a pretty good idea.

'Trouble. With every letter capitalized. First you antagonize the cattlemen by closing their saloon—as they felt it was—and forcing them to drink at our place, if at all, to rub shoulders with sheepmen. That hasn't caused an explosion yet—but it's making a lot of people unhappy.'

'I can imagine.'

'Then you tangle with some of the cattlemen, at heavy odds, and beat them—and that doesn't make them love you any better.'

'I didn't have too much choice.'

'You might have kept out of it, or turned and run—but that wouldn't be your way.' There was a glint of pride in her eyes and voice. 'But it makes them hate you worse, Nels. And if things bust loose in this valley—no, when they do break loose, you'll be right in the middle, with a hardware store.'

He waited, and she went on, suddenly impatient.

'You'll have a supply of guns and ammunition, and both sides will want them—and want to keep them from the other side. It can be bad.'

That was the way he'd figured it, though the thought had never occurred to August, and now it was too late to do anything about it. Nels smiled.

'You're probably right,' he admitted. 'I'm afraid we've done a lot that's wrong. I'm glad to have one real friend, Janie—so long as it's you!'

She colored suddenly, then turned away. 'I don't have too many friends,' she said. 'I'd hate to lose those I have.'

Nels descended to the store the next morning with his gun and belt in place. He had removed them on coming into town, packing them in his bedroll, but now they were in view for all to see. August regarded him with perplexity and yet with a glimmer of understanding.

'What have you in mind?' he asked.

'The stock's pretty well in place, so you can manage here,' Nels pointed out. 'I'll ride out to the Ox-Bow and have a look.'

August nodded slowly. 'I suppose that's necessary,' he conceded. 'But will it be safe? There's a spirit of unrest—and this is a wild land.'

'It has to be done.'

'I suppose so. Be careful, boy.'

'I intend to,' Nels agreed.

He had acquired a working knowledge of

the valley. Not far south from town, where the road forked, the valley widened. The central fork kept almost straight on south, and was the road of the sheepmen, exclusively so. It ran first through Owens' big spread, which lay mostly to the east, then edged west into the adjoining ranch of Delaney. Below those was the property of MacDonald. Short forks of the road west and east and south made connections with the other sheep outfits.

The roads in the valley were like the three tines of a hay fork. The eastern tine swung east by south, through the Rocking Chair, down through the Rafter L and Boxed B. This, like the western fork, was used exclusively by cowboys.

The western road ran through Draine's spread, cut a corner of the Ox-Bow, then down through the Chain, and finally to the K&T. Thus all fourteen ranches were reached, and confrontation between rival outfits avoided, except in town.

Thunderman River rolled down from the north, feeding the Ox-Bow, swinging south and east to vanish finally beyond the Box B. Lesser streams which were tributaries made the whole valley prosperous.

'And if one man could get hold of the whole valley, that would be something,' Nels reflected. 'Which was what Bart was aiming at. Somebody liked his plan and aimed to take over, first getting him out of the way. And who would know more about what Bart planned than his lawyer?'

There was logic in this reasoning, but a lot of factors did not fit. Of the factors which he knew, the first was that Bart had preferred to work from under cover, and to absent himself from the Valley of the Gun, until such time as his brother-in-law and nephew should arrive, to trigger the planned explosion.

There had been changes, but the potentialities remained the same. And if Bart had been in the way of others, then Nels, as Bart's nephew, intent on prying, would be even more so.

The risk entailed now in merely staying alive was considerable, and was enhanced by his taking an active part. Yet the only way was to bring matters into the open. Otherwise, Crockett would have been able to do as he pleased. The chief hindrance had probably been what had happened to Hennessey. The foreman had almost certainly been working for Crockett since Bart's demise. Had he been working for the lawyer prior to that?

He rode with the knowledge that forcing a showdown could be playing into the hands of Bart's enemies, who now were his as well. Murder was a weapon, and it could be used to trigger the conflict which was necessary to the execution of the over-all plan. In that, sheepmen would seek earnestly to annihilate cattlemen, with the cowboys doing the same in their turn. The more thorough the job, the easier it would be for the watcher from the shadows to pick up the pieces, once the carnage was ended.

Here the road divided, and his course lay along the western fork, toward the Ox-Bow. To reach it, he'd be riding for miles through Draine's land. Nels swung off from the wheel-trace, discreetly to the side and out of sight.

He'd covered several miles when sounds drew him back toward the road. They were confused noises, but unmistakably denoted trouble.

The roadway narrowed and crowded close, hemmed between evergreens. Men on horses surrounded a big wagon, after the manner of ants who had entrapped a beetle. The high-piled load was being removed, tumbled over the side, while the driver sat helplessly, menaced by a pair of leveled guns. Nels blinked in surprised recognition. What was Floyd Clayton doing way North in cattle country, and driving a wagon?

Nor was Clayton the only acquaintance. Sue MacDonald was standing, forcibly restrained by two men who held her arms. The angry blood surged beneath her skin, and she gave a sudden desperate wrench in an effort to break free. One of her captors grinned.

'Whoa now, Sue, take it easy. You ain't going anywhere—not right now!'

CHAPTER FIFTEEN

Larch Draine was the speaker, and he was obviously in charge. That he should be there was not too surprising, since this land belonged to the Draines. Today, there was no sign of the Van Sickles, but that was not surprising, either. Their range was a long way south and east from there.

One man had been busily tossing boxes and sacks from the wagon, with a careless disregard for breakage. He paused to wipe sweat from his face, then turned a questioning, somewhat puzzled look on Draine.

'I don't quite get this,' he protested. 'Why don't we just leave the stuff in the wagon and take it somewhere, use it ourselves, Larch? Seems a shame to waste all this good grub.'

Most of the goods were foodstuffs; there were sacks of flour and beans, along with canned goods, coffee and sides of bacon. Most of them had been thrown into a pit-like hole below the road.

Larch shook his head, his mouth set stubbornly. 'You want to eat sheepherders' grub?' he asked bitingly. 'We ain't come to that yet. Throw out the rest.'

Resignedly, the two who were unloading the wagon tugged at a heavy crate. In sudden desperation, Clayton spun around, snatching for the whip, in its socket at the corner of the wagon box. It came clear, but before he could bring it into play, Larch jumped his horse ahead, lashing out with the barrel of his revolver while Clayton's back was turned. The vicious swipe of the steel caught him alongside the head, and Floyd slumped onto the seat, then collapsed into the bottom of the wagon.

Sue cried out, again struggling frantically. 'You inhuman beast!' she railed. 'You murderer!'

Larch turned a mocking eye on her, while her captors held her fast.

'You asked yourself to this party, Sue,' he reminded her, 'trespassin' where sheepmen have got no business to come. Get on with the job,' he added, then jerked about, gun leveling nervously as Nels rode into sight.

It might be foolhardy to intervene against such odds, but these people were his friends, and Nels knew what he was doing; at least he hoped so. When setting out on a journey which would certainly be risky, he had made certain preparations, along with some precautions.

Something of apprehension clouded

Larch's eyes for a moment; then it was replaced by a taunting triumph.

'Well, look who's back!' he gloated. 'Stickin' his nose into what's none of his business one more time—and I reckon it'll be the last! Which suits us just fine, Ondane.'

'You keep at the same sort of work, don't you?' Nels shrugged. 'Your family seem to have a liking for murder.'

The crew had suspended operations, watching. The news of this man's past encounters with the Draines, father and son, was widely known. Sue MacDonald's eyes were wide, her breathing hurried. Floyd Clayton stirred. The horses, pawing uneasily, were prevented from bolting by the men who held the girl.

'Murder?' Larch returned thinly. 'Some killings ain't murder—not when you get rid of varmints! But it strikes me that you're a bigger fool than I took you for, ridin' into something like this. You've been lucky a time or so, but there's a limit to luck.'

'Why, now, I'll have to agree with you there,' Nels drawled. 'So don't crowd yours too far.'

Larch studied him sharply, uneasy despite the odds which seemed so overwhelmingly in his favor. But it had been that way when Ondane had tangled with his father, making even the old wolf look bad. Ondanes were always dangerous.

'Just what do you think you're going to do, now that you're here?' he taunted 'Stop a bullet?'

Nels had considered appearing with his own gun drawn, making full use of surprise; the trouble was that he doubted the outcome of such a showdown, and Sue and Floyd were involved in this, as well as himself. He was fairly good with a gun, but certainly no match for these cowboys. He might be lucky and disarm them, but the probability was that they'd be desperate enough for a shoot-out. If that happened, the skill, and probably the luck, would be on their side.

His lariat was tied at one side of the saddle. Opposite it was a coiled blacksnake, the long whip loose and resting under his hand, largely out of sight.

What none of these people suspected was his expertness with a bullwhip, gained in working back East at odd intervals as a muleskinner. Without warning, he sent the whip writhing out. The end of the lash closed about Larch's wrist, and a quick jerk flicked the gun from his grip and into the road. Draine cried out in pain, staring incredulously at his wrist.

An instant later, the writhing tip of the lash was dancing before the eyes of the pair who held the girl, causing them to loose their hold and jump back in terror.

Sue took instant advantage of the

opportunity. She darted forward and snatched the holstered gun from the belt of the nearer guard, then swung to menace both with it. The pair on the wagon watched, bewildered, not at all anxious for trouble.

Nels hid a grin, recalling how explosively Sue had greeted him on their first encounter.

'Better dehorn them all round, Sue,' he suggested.

'I intend to,' she assured him, and moved with no lost motion to get their guns. Within moments, all five had been disarmed, and at a motion of the whip, they huddled together where they could be more easily watched. As soon as she was sure that they were safely under control, Sue hastened to Floyd, exclaiming as she bent over him.

Clayton sat up uncertainly, steadied by her arm. 'I'm all right,' he assured her. 'Doing fine, with him to look out for me. I don't know how I'd manage without you turnin' up at such times, Nels,' he added.

Sue's smile was equally grateful. 'You certainly have a way of doing things,' she agreed. 'We can never thank you enough.'

Though curious as to what they were doing on that road, in that part of the valley, Nels did not ask questions. What to do with them, as well as with the prisoners, was of more immediate concern. The sound of approaching horsemen, coming along the road though still out of sight, added to the dilemma.

Recognizing the risk, Sue swung about, gun in hand, passing another to Clayton, who propped himself in a corner of the wagon box. A pair of riders came into sight, halting in surprise. The younger man was one of the Van Sickle brothers, and a look at the older, with his close resemblance, assured Nels that he was the senior Van Sickle himself.

The older man looked about keenly, studying Nels momentarily, then shifting his regard to Sue. He did not seem at all concerned about the guns which menaced him, and after a moment, Sue looked uncertain. Gravely, he tipped his hat to her.

'Would you mind explaining what this is all about, Miss Sue?' he asked. 'What's Larch been up to now?'

'I think Larch has gotten off on the wrong foot, Mr. Van Sickle, with some foolish notions that someone else must have given him,' Sue explained. 'He and these others jumped Floyd here, and were destroying his load, threatening to kill him, until Mr. Ondane happened along.'

Larch Draine flushed, then lost color under Van Sickle's sharp regard, but said nothing. Van Sickle looked curiously at Nels.

'So you're Nels Ondane,' he observed. 'I've been hearing of you. You seem to be living up to your reputation!'

'He ain't nothing like Bart Ondane,' Larch

cut in. 'He always sides with the sheepmen!'

'I don't approve of robbery and murder,' Nels returned flatly, 'which seems to be somewhat of a habit with some folks.'

'He's got you there, Larch,' Van Sickle remarked dryly. 'You've been running with the wrong crowd. But I still don't quite know what this is all about.'

'Neither do I,' Nels admitted. 'But they were holding Sue and Floyd as prisoners, and throwing off that load, when I came along.'

Sue looked at Van Sickle with a mixture of defiance and appeal.

'Maybe we've no right to be off here on this road,' she admitted. 'But after all, a road is a road. Floyd was taking supplies down it to beyond the North Fork, where there's a passable road across to McClure graze. It's almost impossible to get in there any other way, with the sort of blockade that's been thrown up against us the last few weeks.'

Even without the blockade, the long way around would be the easiest, with mountains rearing forbiddingly between that part of the sheepmen's range and the end of their road. Clayton had decided to take a chance, using the cattlemen's road, to supply isolated herders. Larch spoke angrily.

'That's what we were stopping them for, Uncle George. They've got no right to use our road!'

'We have too got a right,' Clayton blazed.

'This is a county road, not a private one. Anybody's got a right to it.'

'You've found out,' Larch said sullenly.

'He's right.' Van Sickle nodded wearily. 'It is a county road, and by rights, open to all. Who's been putting you up to all this trouble-making, Larch? I can understand your Dad—he's always sort of proddy—but I thought better of you. Who's been bugging you?'

'I don't need any bugging,' Larch returned sullenly. 'I can think for myself.'

'Then it's about time you started to do some thinking! You got my boys into a mess the other day, though maybe they were as much at fault as you. But you're my sister's son, and she means a lot to me, and so does the rest of the family. So I'm asking you a question, and I want a straight answer. Whose side are you on?'

Larch looked bewildered, then uncomfortable.

'Why—why, I'm on your side, Uncle George,' he stammered. 'I didn't think there was any difference—'

'I suppose you didn't think very much about it,' his uncle returned wearily. 'Some folks in this valley are out to make trouble, using the rest of us as cat's-paws. I can't see things that way. We've lived together a good many years in this country, cattlemen and sheepmen, and we'll have to keep right on living as neighbors, or everybody loses. Load up what you've thrown out,' he ordered the crewmen. 'After that, Clayton, you can go on as you'd planned.'

He watched speculatively for a moment as the others obeyed willingly enough, then came to a fresh conclusion.

'I want that load to go through without further molestation. So, Larch, you'll go along with Floyd, you and Tom here riding shotgun. See that he gets through safely!'

The cousins looked uncertain, and Larch swallowed. Then he met his uncle's eyes and straightened.

'We'll see that he gets through,' he promised.

One of the men who had been holding Sue at the beginning looked incredulous.

'You mean that you're sending them along to guard a sheepherder's outfit?' he demanded. 'Now I've seen everything!'

'You haven't—yet,' Van Sickle warned grimly. 'I expect you'll streak straight to your boss and give him an account of this, Hasp, and that's your right. But if you or anyone else interfere with either of them, you'll have me to settle with. I'm tired of this foolishness, and so far as I'm concerned, it's got to stop.'

Nels spoke, surprised but grateful.

'That's what we all need, a reasonable attitude,' he agreed. 'Give them back their guns, Sue. I'm heading for Ox-Bow, which I figure still belongs to the Ondanes. And speaking in the capacity of owners, we'd like nothing better than to get along on good terms with our neighbors—all of them.'

The supplies had been reloaded, and Floyd seemed sufficiently recovered to handle the reins again. Sue eyed him anxiously, then extended her hands, one to Nels, the other to Van Sickle.

'I'm grateful to both of you,' she said, 'especially you, Nels. But I think I'd better go on with Floyd, to make sure that he's all right.'

A chastened pair of cousins prepared to ride on. Nels was beginning to understand why Clayton continued to work for Sue's father, despite the risk. He had a propensity for blundering into trouble, but he certainly was not lacking in courage. Also, there was the matter of personal interest, where Sue was concerned. It was like the stab of an unexpected cactus for Nels to recognize it.

It's easy to see why Floyd keeps working for MacDonald, no matter how rough a job it is, he thought. And Sue appreciates what he's doing, which I guess is all right and proper. They're both friends of mine, and they deserve the best.

The words were easy enough to form in his mind, but to accept them came hard. Nels rode on, his attention divided, striking off through the tree country. He was roused from his uneasy abstraction by the terrified bleat of a calf.

It was a very young calf, left hidden by its mother among the grass and now struggling belatedly and unsteadily to its feet, terrified by a sudden rank whiff of danger in its nostrils, a lengthening shadow from the limb of a tree above. Even as Nels saw the puma, it started its leap, and he jerked frantically for his revolver.

CHAPTER SIXTEEN

To catch and check the puma in mid-air would have been good shooting for anyone, better than Nels had any hope of managing with his limited skill. The gun cleared leather with commendable speed, but he was not surprised when he failed to score a hit, though the gun's blast was almost as useful. At the explosion, the startled predator almost literally changed course, twisting in mid-leap, as frightened as its intended victim had been an instant before. The diversion, while not much, was enough. Outreaching paws hit the ground to the side of where it had aimed; then the big cat went streaking for deeper cover.

There was no time for a second shot. The calf, terrified and still wobbly, blundered into a thicket of bushes and stopped. But help was at hand. The old cow, bawling defiance and reassurance, emerged at a run from another thicket, then over her offspring, glaring at the horseman. She nuzzled it reassuringly, then moved away.

'That was a close call all around, old girl,' Nels muttered. 'But maybe you'll keep a closer watch from now on.' He was preparing to ride on when another gun-shot jangled his nerves. The sound came from somewhere back along the road, one blast, not repeated. It seemed to carry the suggeston of disaster.

Nels hesitated. Whatever it might connote, it was probably none of his business, and it would undoubtedly be more prudent to keep on as though he had not heard. But already the perverse streak in him was taking over as he pulled his horse around.

The scene as he returned to the road was different, yet about it was a deadly familiarity. A riderless horse grazed with dragging reins at the rim of the road; while it snatched at the grass, it rolled its eyes uneasily at the prone figure which had tumbled from the saddle and lay some distance away. Nels needed only a glance to be certain that this was the horse that Van Sickle had been riding.

The man was Van Sickle, and he did not stir at Nels' approach. There was a still bleeding wound, both in his back and chest, where a bullet had passed entirely through his body. Studying its mute evidence, Nels saw that it had been fired into his back.

Judging by the force and penetration of the bullet, it must have been from a rifle, with the bushwhacker remaining carefully out of sight. This was a deliberate furthering of the plan for the valley, implementing terror through cold-blooded murder.

And one of the group whom Van Sickle had harangued only minutes before must have fired the shot, making him a victim because he had spoken out for justice and fair play. Van Sickle had been too much of a man to go along blindly with his own class in a war against the sheepmen. This was his reward, swift and ruthless.

Sickened as much by the act as by the slowly clotting blood, Nels dropped to a knee for a closer look. There was nothing that he could do for Van himself; death had been instant. But if there was any evidence as to who had done this—

It came to him that he was equally exposed and just as vulnerable to attack as Van Sickle had been; also, there was a better than even chance that the gunman might be still in the vicinity, perhaps considering if he should add one more notch to his tally. A man who had just killed in such fashion was not likely to have any compunctions in regard to another.

There was a sudden clatter of hoofs, and

Nels jumped to his feet as a trio of horsemen swept around a bend of the road. It was not unreasonable, of course, that they too should have heard the shot and be coming to investigate. One was Hasp, who had accepted Van Sickle's interference at the wagon with poor grace. Flanking him on one side was Crockett; Draine was opposite. Crockett was new to the scene, but he did not seem out of place in such company.

Draine pulled to a sliding stop, his scowl dark but uncertain. 'What's this?' he demanded, and jumped down, crossing over to have a closer look at the fallen man. Rage thickened his voice as he straightened. 'Murder!' he said tightly.

'I'm afraid you're right,' Nels agreed. 'I heard the shot, and came to have a look. I found him this way.'

'I'll bet you did!' Hasp's voice dripped sarcasm. 'A man could hardly help hearing his own gun! That being so, let's just have a look at yours.'

He held out his hand, the gesture peremptory. Nels hesitated, then handed it over. Here was the old pattern, repeated with an added note of grimness. He'd made the mistake first of coming to the bait, then being caught. That Van Sickle's death was bait for a trap, and that it had been set for him, he could scarcely doubt. The pattern of events both past and to come was emerging with ever greater clarity.

To resist would be playing their game. They would welcome an excuse to get him out of the picture, just as had been done with Van Sickle.

Hasp took the gun, broke it open, sighted through the barrel, then sniffed at the muzzle. 'New-fired, minutes ago,' he observed, and handed it on to Draine for confirmation.

'Seems to be an open and shut case,' Draine agreed briefly. 'We ought to string him up.' He looked slantwise at the lawyer. 'Or would you insist on our observin' a lot of fool forms?'

Crockett shrugged, then spread his hands in a disarming gesture.

'I know how you fellows feel,' he admitted. 'So do I, when it comes to that. But we're not barbarians, and we can't afford to be the ones to touch off a war here in the valley.' Nels had no doubt that he was speaking for the record. 'I think that we should take him to the Ox-Bow and lock him up, for the present.'

Draine's already thin lips creased to a straight line. 'An eye for an eye and a tooth for a tooth,' he quoted angrily. 'Why waste time?'

'I'm afraid I couldn't agree to drastic action—not at this time,' Crockett insisted. 'We might be making a mistake.'

'If we waste time, that'll be the mistake,' Draine grunted. But when Hasp voted with Crockett, he reluctantly agreed to follow the suggestion. Nels was wondering, since its logical furtherance would have been to take him in to town, not the ranch.

Hasp knotted a length of rawhide around Nels' wrists, jerking his hands behind his back, and tied it painfully tightly. He assisted him roughly to mount his horse again, exchanging an understanding glance with the lawyer, which Draine did not see.

'Somebody has to look after Van Sickle,' Hasp suggested. 'Ought to take him in to town and report what happened.' He addressed himself to Draine, who shrugged moodily.

'All right; I'll tend to it,' he agreed.

They assisted Draine in loading the dead man onto his own horse and tying him fast for his last ride. Then Draine set out, leading the burdened animal. Crockett and Hasp swung toward the Ox-Bow. Nels caught the satisfied grin on both their faces as Draine's back was turned.

They rode in silence, single-file, Nels' horse between the others. He considered whether to protest or argue, but decided that it would be a waste of breath. There seemed little doubt that this was also his last ride, or at least they planned for it to be.

Draine had been a handy tool, a willing

accomplice, but Nels doubted that he was included in the important planning. That by now was becoming clear enough; each piece of the pattern was falling into place. The original notion had been Bart Ondane's, and he had worked patiently, not scrupling to use his own kin as instruments of policy.

It had seemed necessary for him to disappear for a while and be reported dead, so that his heirs could inherit the saloon and, with August so bitterly opposed to liquor in all its forms, take some rash action which would precipitate a crisis and trigger violence.

Once begun, that was to spread in a flame of destruction. After it had run its course, Bart Ondane would return, to straddle the valley like a giant, reaping the fruits of other men's folly.

The weak link in his planning had been that he must work a part of it through a lawyer, and he had miscalculated when choosing Crockett as his instrument. Crockett too could play a part, but he was not the weak sister that he had appeared. He had been quick to grasp the possibilities in the plan, then had taken steps to remove Bart Ondane. Though he remained in the background, Nels was convinced that it was he who now pulled the strings.

Ox-Bow, like many things connected with Bart Ondane, was a surprise. The buildings were located in a narrow valley, and an irrigation ditch came down from the hills above and ran just below them. Apparently it carried water from a creek to land otherwise dry and worthless. Just now, the ditch ran bank full.

A few buildings of a bygone day remained below the ditch, fallen to ruin. Those above it were well-painted, with a prosperous look. Observing these details, Nels was conscious of a growing respect for his uncle. Wherever he had turned his talents to constructive purposes, Bart had shown real ability. His life-long obsession about getting even, settling fancied grudges against his fellows, had been his one great weakness.

They followed an old road below the ditch, and paused at the lawyer's suggestion. Beside the road yawned a hole, a pit-like opening a dozen feet deep. The sides looked smooth and sheer.

'I think we might be safer if we put him in there for safekeeping temporarily,' Crockett suggested. 'There's no one around to keep watch on him, but that'll hold him. He couldn't climb those sides, even if he wasn't tied. So he'll be here when wanted.'

Hasp was so ready to do that Nels' suspicions were confirmed. He found another rawhide thong and used it to fasten his ankles together. Then they lowered him, not too gently, allowing him to drop part way to the bottom of the hole. The sound of diminishing hoofbeats thereafter indicated that they must have urgent business elsewhere.

Nels twisted on to his back, then, wriggling and hitching, managed to prop himself against the side and look around. What he could see was not encouraging. There was nothing against which he might rub or catch his bonds in an effort to loosen them. Even if he should get loose from the thongs, Crockett's estimation appeared accurate. It would be virtually impossible to climb out unassisted, and to jump high enough was out of the question.

Should he try calling for help, there was only a remote chance he would be heard. Crockett had said that the ranch buildings were deserted, and even if anyone should come around and hear, they would probably belong to his crew and refuse to assist him.

For want of anything better to do, he strained against the cords, wriggling and twisting, but they were well tied, drawn much too tight to give.

Yet if he was to escape, it was probably now or never. It was easy to guess what was scheduled to happen in the valley, and he was a part of the whole. The takeover was about to begin, and a bloody climax was in the making.

Perhaps Crockett was hindered by a sense of public ethics which would not have caused Bart a moment's concern. He was ostensibly to remain aloof, to profit only after catastrophe had had its way. As a lawyer, he would give lip service to the law.

A thin streak of sunlight reached the bottom of the hole, and insects buzzed near the surface. Otherwise the silence was profound. Then a new sound attracted Nels' attention, and the sunlight took on a brighter sheen, reflected on water. Staring in disbelief, Nels saw that it was water, a trickle splashing down into the hole at the side opposite from him, like a miniature waterfall.

Even as he watched the stream grew in size, already forming a pool along the bottom, beginning to spread out. Within moments it was lapping at his feet, while the volume of the stream was steadily increasing.

After the initial surprise, he understood well enough. Someone, very likely Crockett, had taken time to insert a board in a flood-gate somewhere along the ditch. That was blocking off enough water to cause an overflow at a low point of the ditch, somewhere up above. The spill was finding its way to the lowest point at hand, this hole below the ditch.

Already the bottom was covered, so that he was being gradually immersed. He viewed the rising water grimly, but with a countervailing hope. The plan of his enemies was simple enough. As the hole filled, they probably figured that, tied hand and foot, he would drown. What would appear to anyone to have been a chance break in the ditch would make a convenient accident.

What they had overlooked and could not very well know was that he was at home in the water. Even with hands and feet tied, he could float quite easily. So there seemed a fair chance that the rising water would finally hoist him to the top, where he might wash or crawl free of the trap. The process would probably be a chilly one before that point was reached, but that could not be helped.

The scheme was working as Crockett must have planned, and also as he hoped. Soon the water was deep enough so that he was floating, lifted off the bottom. The stream at the side continued unabated. He estimated that a couple of hours would be required to fill the hole to the top, but the water, having coursed for some distance along the ditch, was not so cold as it might have been.

Gradually the pool was deepening, lifting him as the level rose. There was an additional dividend which his captors had forgotten or failed to understand. As the rawhide thongs soaked, they began to stretch. It was an ordeal to wait patiently for the soaking to take effect. The water seemed colder as he soaked along with the rawhide. Finally, struggling, he was able to slip one hand loose. Then, splashing and maneuvering in the water, he got his feet untied as well.

That was a tremendous relief, as well as benefit, in being able to swim. He threshed about, and the exercise helped warm him. It shouldn't be long now until the inrushing stream would fill the pit high enough for him to be able to reach the top and scramble out—

Then, circling the pool, he made an unpleasant discovery. For the last several minutes, the water mark had not crept up. The upper half of the walls were far too sheer and smooth to afford any sort of grip or hold for climbing, but from this elevation there was something that he had overlooked while prone on the bottom. A crack or crevice was in one wall, and through that the water was escaping, pouring back out as fast as it entered at the top.

That drain, unguessed and unexpected, was holding him trapped. The top was just a few feet away, barely beyond reach; still, it was as hopelessly removed as when he'd been on the bottom. A few desperate attempts to emulate a trout or porpoise and leap upward demonstrated the impossibility.

Worse, the long immersion was bringing an increasing chill. He could fight it only so long by violent exercise. Then cold and exhaustion would take their toll. After that, whether seized with cramps or merely played out, he'd drown exactly as his captors had intended.

CHAPTER SEVENTEEN

August surveyed the well-stocked store with a strong pride of possession. Here was a dream come true. That it was a dream which had always eluded him until it had seemed impossible of attainment, made it all the more satisfying.

'And the best part is that there's no taint to a good honest hardware business,' he muttered aloud. 'Such a stock as we have here does not carry the seeds of destruction in itself, as does the demon rum. Where such a product tears down, these goods will build a community. A man behind a plow, or using a hammer and saw to make a house—'

He broke off and turned at the opening of the door, pleased to see a trio of customers. He felt a momentary uneasiness as he recognized Draine, remembering their previous meeting; but today the cattleman was sober and seemed in a good mood. He introduced his companions.

'Mr. Ondane, I'd like you to meet Ford and Tooker. You and I know each other already, and I will say this: it takes a good man to handle me as you did.'

'No hard feelings,' August suggested. 'There was nothing personal in it.'

'Of course not. I'd had a bit too much to

drink, just as you said.' He looked about appraisingly, clearly searching for the right words. 'This is a nice store. Just what we needed.'

'I'm glad you think so.'

'I certainly do. And we're here to make some purchases. You said something about needing another saddle, Jerry.'

Ford nodded. All three had a curious listening attitude; it was as though they held themselves with a tight rein. 'One of my boys got shucked off his horse, way back miles from anywhere,' he explained. 'Saddle and all. Broken cinch. He walked in, but didn't pack it along. When he went back, an old grizzly had made a plaything of that piece of leather. After that, it wasn't worth bringing back.'

He selected a saddle, including a pair of spurs, then added a blanket, almost as an afterthought. From the street came the sounds of voices, of men and vehicles. Tooker bought a buggy-whip and a new gun-belt. He strapped on the belt, then eyed the empty loops with a wry smile.

'This won't do,' he protested. 'Give me a box of forty-five cartridges. I'd feel plumb undressed, going about this way.'

He opened the box, stuffing shells into the empty loops until they bristled with shiny brass. Draine watched, still with the air of holding tight against a desperate need for hurry.

'When it comes to that, we might as well stock up on cartridges, too,' he suggested. 'I'm running kind of low back on the ranch, and these are good and fresh. How many have you got on hand, Ondane?'

August flushed at the name, but did not remind them that it was not his name. He made a quick calculation. 'About thirty boxes of revolver shells.'

'We'll take them, divide them between us. Save running in for a fresh supply all the time.'

'All the time? You sound as though you used a lot of them.'

'It varies,' Draine returned carelessly. 'Sometimes with hunting and so on, we do, and then again, a man won't bust a cap for weeks. But it's handier to have plenty of them on hand. And I'll take some rifle shells, too. You got plenty?'

'Thirty-thirties and 303's. And some twenty-twos.'

'Put them all in. Those are the calibers we use.'

August swung back in amazement. 'You don't mean all that I've got on hand?'

'Sure. Why not? They'll come in handy, sooner or later.'

August stared, listening to the confusion from outside, which seemed to be mounting. He was suddenly uneasy.

'I can let you have a reasonable supply,' he decided, 'up to half of what I've got in stock. But not more than that. I have to think of other customers. I'll order more, and have all you want within a short while, so it'll amount to the same thing.'

Tooker's face flooded red. 'When we give an order, we want it filled just the way we say, and now, not some other time,' he snapped.

'Yeah, we're here to buy, cash on the barrelhead,' Ford seconded him. 'If anybody has to wait, it can be the late-comers.'

August's head-shake was decisive. 'I'm sorry, gentlemen,' he said. 'But you can see for yourselves that such a course wouldn't be either fair or good business. This is the only store of its kind anywhere around, and there are as many cattlemen as sheepmen in the valley, or vice-versa. I aim to be both fair and neutral, treating everyone alike. You wouldn't like it if I sold exclusively to the sheepmen, and they'd have an equally just complaint if I sold everything to you.'

'Then they can complain,' Draine snapped. 'We want those cartridges, every one you have in the store. And we want them now!'

'But I tell you I can't sell you more than half—'

'Mister,' Tooker warned ominously, 'you don't have any choice. We're here to buy, and we're buying! Better make sure you stay on our good side, for from now on, there won't be any problem of sheep or sheepmen in this country. Just cattlemen.'

'That's right,' Draine added. 'I just brought in a friend of mine that the sheepmen murdered. We're puttin' a stop to that.' He swung, gun in hand, as the door burst open again.

* * *

A combination of caution, pride and doubt had kept Nels silent as he took turns floating or swimming. It had seemed that there was a chance for escape if he worked quietly; in any case, such ears as might possibly be around to hear any calls for help would almost certainly be hostile, rather than friendly.

Now, with the discovery that the pool was draining as fast as it filled, and with the penetrating chill making his movements sluggish, he tried yelling, not hopefully, but out of desperation. Cramps could send him to the bottom of the pool, so if there was nothing to gain, neither was there anything to lose.

To his amazement, there came an answering call; then, moments later, Sue MacDonald burst into sight above, staring down with an amazement almost equal to his own. It took her only an instant to understand the situation, and she darted away, returning promptly to toss the loop of a lariat to him. Nels grasped the rope. With her assistance, he managed to climb out onto the bank.

He was shivering violently, scarcely able to stand. Sue gave him a hand, slipping an arm about his shoulders as he staggered.

'You'll get all soaked,' he protested. 'Golly, am I glad to see you!'

She disregarded his wetness, stepping out briskly. 'You need dry clothes and a chance to get warm,' she returned practically. 'Let's see what we can find.'

There was a bridge across the ditch; then they headed for the buildings. Exercise had a warming effect, and Nels hesitated.

'There may be somebody around,' he pointed out. 'We'd better not disturb them if we can help it.'

'Let's try the bunkhouse,' Sue suggested. 'It's pretty sure to be empty, this time of day.'

Her guess proved correct. After a quick glance about the murky interior, she left him at the door.

'You can help yourself to some dry clothes. I'll keep watch while you change.'

Nels lost no time before availing himself of the opportunity, selecting from garments which were a reasonably good fit. Their owners might throw a fit of their own when they discovered the exchange, but that was all right. Dry again, he was shaking off the chill, more in a mood for whatever might come. One thing was disappointing. He could find no gun in the bunkhouse.

He saw a thin streamer of smoke rising from the chimney of the main house as he stepped outside. Then Sue came to the door and beckoned to him.

'I had a look, and there's nobody around,' she explained. 'So I'm taking the liberty of cooking a meal for us. We both need it.'

There was an aroma of frying beefsteak and boiling coffee. The latter was the perennial pot, warmed over and bitter, but its bite was welcome. Sue indicated an adjoining room.

'That looks like an office,' she said. 'Maybe you can find a gun, while I dish up the food.'

Nels nodded, draining the cup of coffee which she had poured for him. He found a six-shooter in a desk drawer, and once it was strapped on, felt better.

'I'll soon think and feel like I belonged in this country—if I live long enough,' he reflected, as the meal was ready.

'How did you happen along just when I needed you?' he asked.

'I heard the shooting and turned back,' Sue explained. 'I decided that the others would manage nicely without me. Later, I saw horsemen heading this way, and while I couldn't make out who they were, it seemed like this might be a good place to come.'

She added matter-of-factly. 'I'm glad I could. You've had a way of turning up when I needed help.'

That was her reason, and she had more than repaid any debt which might have existed. Nels checked the rush of words which threatened to pour out. If he tried to thank her, he'd probably say too much.

He could no longer hide from himself how he felt about her. Wild as the notion would have seemed a few days before, he not only admired the daughter of a sheepman, but had fallen wildly in love with her. It was the sort of experience of which he had sometimes dreamed, a development in life which he had expected would be both satisfying and exciting.

The trouble as it had been easy to see, was that this was just a matter of business. He knew where her thoughts centered, and it was not on him.

'What happened after you left me?' she asked. 'How did you get in such a fix?'

He explained about Van Sickle, and what had followed. Sue's face was grave.

'You've been trying to help whoever happened to be the underdog, and now they are afraid of you,' she said. 'You've interfered with big plans, so they'll do anything to be rid of you. I'm frightened.'

'I am, too,' Nels admitted. 'I think they're ready for the big blow-off, and in any case, the lid's likely to pop of its own accord. I think we should get to your people and let them know what's going on as soon as we can. After that, there may be a chance to bring matters under control. But it has to be done before everybody starts shooting.'

'You're right,' she agreed. 'We'd better get moving.'

Her own horse was where she had left it, and Nels found saddle ponies in the barn. He helped himself to one; then, with Sue leading the way, they set off.

'I hope we're in time,' she said anxiously. 'But we have pretty much to go it blind. I know that both groups are gathering, expecting trouble. But where any of them may be is a matter for guesswork. If we get to them in time, maybe you can manage. If we should miss them—'

Time, of course, could be the key. As they rode, the great valley seemed deserted except for themselves, with no sound to break the brooding stillness. It was a silence which might erupt with the potency of a long-dormant volcano.

CHAPTER EIGHTEEN

As if in answer to the fear which gripped them, sound came, booming from the distance, the irregular tom-tom of guns. New as this kind of thing was to him, Nels could assess the gravity of the situation by the uneven spacing of the shots. Had game been the target, there would be a more precise pattern.

Sue glanced at him, her face strained, listening with her head cocked to the side. It was a wholly unconscious gesture, at once demure and provocative.

'That firing comes from somewhere in the Hollow, I think,' she explained. 'If we circle, we can approach from above them and see what the situation is.'

The gunfire continued sporadically as they kept on, its nature suggesting opposing groups which were engaged in feeling each other out. The Hollow itself, as she explained, was by way of being disputed territory, a borderland where both sheep and cattle grazed at times. It was a deep valley in a rough and broken section, one of many such bones of contention.

Sue proved an excellent guide. They circled along a hillside, cut through deep forest, ascended a barren knoll, and came out on a height where they could look down. As expected, there were two groups of men, combatants each occupying a good defensive position, each harassing the other. Those deepest in the Hollow were obviously sheepmen, exchanging an occasional shot with cowboys of about equal strength, who were no more than a quarter of a mile from where Sue and Nels crouched. From their vantage-point, the cattlemen could keep the others pinned down, though to get at them or inflict much damage might be a costly procedure. For the moment, the situation was a stand-off.

Off at the side, not seeming to be bothered by the guns, a herd of cattle grazed.

'Isn't there something that we can do?' Sue asked. 'Yet I suppose they'd be mighty stubborn, on both sides, and turn on us if we tried to stop them.'

Since that was usually the fate of the peace-maker, Nels was in agreement. Yet some sort of action was imperative, as the developing situation could only worsen.

Already it was becoming apparent that the cattlemen, disliking the stalemate but with little stomach for carrying the battle to so well entrenched an enemy, were considering a countermove. Three of them had started to work back, away from the battle. Presently, reaching their horses, out of sight of possible gunfire, they mounted and headed toward the grazing herd.

'What do you think they're up to?' Sue asked uneasily. Her sympathies, quite naturally, were with her own people.

Nels was afraid that he understood. The sheepmen, apparently taken by surprise in the initial encounter, had been able to take cover in a good defensive position. So long as the opposing force remained relatively equal, they could hardly be routed or hurt save at heavy cost. But there was one serious weakness in their position.

The three cowboys were circling to get beyond the cattle, already starting to push outlying animals toward a compact herd. Nels pointed this out.

'I think they plan to get the herd moving, then stampede them,' he explained. 'Once they're on the run, they'd head right over and through your folks.'

Sue caught her breath sharply. Such a scheme, with a large herd conveniently at hand, was entirely feasible. The natural slope of the ground would funnel a running bunch straight at the defenders, to burst upon them almost without warning. Several hundred head, plunging along wildly, would render the position untenable. The herders would have to run for their lives, and when that happened, they would be exposed to the withering fire of their enemies. At best it would be a rout, and might easily become a slaughter.

Sue bit her lip, her face twisting agonizingly. 'What are we going to do?' she asked. 'I feel like shooting some of them, only that would be murder! But that's what they intend.'

'And that's what we must prevent, somehow,' Nels returned. 'If it ever gets to that stage, anywhere in the valley, then nothing can stop the war until it has spread from one end to the other.' That, of course, was what had been planned, a cold-blooded slaughter leaving chaos in its wake.

'Do you think we can stop them?' she asked.

So far, the sheepmen were not aware of any change in the situation, since they could not see the cattle or guess what was being prepared against them. When the stampede got under way, it would sweep at them so suddenly that they would be unprepared.

'There's a chance that we can scare the herd and turn them enough to miss,' Nels agreed, pointing out the obvious. 'I'll ride at them suddenly when they break past those trees, and you fire a few shots to send the bullets zooming just above their noses. That ought to do it.'

Sue had been thinking along the same lines, since nothing else could help. She nodded agreement.

'Fine; only you couldn't manage alone. Both of us together may be able to. I'll ride with you.'

He had expected such an answer, knowing Sue as he did. It would improve the chance for success, but at the same time it was highly dangerous.

'No, Sue, I don't want you to do that,' he protested. 'If anything should happen to you—'

Briefly, but as warmingly as a flash of sunlight, her smile touched him, pleased but unswerving.

'Why should you take all the risk?' she asked. 'Those are my people, not yours. I won't be in any more danger than you are.'

'But you're a woman,' he blurted. 'The cowboys will be mad, and they may not pay much attention who they shoot at—'

'I won't let you go alone,' she returned with finality. 'Together we may be able to work it. Alone, you wouldn't stand a chance.'

Her logic was past refuting, and in any case, much more than the immediate issue rode on this venture. Failure now would make the war inevitable. Once such a struggle ravaged the valley, women and children were almost certain to be among the casualties.

'All right,' he agreed. 'If you will, we'll have to chance it.' Thoughtfully he removed his coat. 'I'll wave this in their faces when the cattle come along. But you don't have anything—'

Sue's face turned a bright scarlet as she met his eyes, but a glint of humor showed in them.

'Don't worry; I'll have something to wave, too,' she promised, and stepped behind a screen of brush. When she returned, he saw that she had removed an underskirt, which would serve as a flag to flaunt in the eyes of the terrified cattle.

They mounted their horses, taking their positions. The remaining cowboys were moving back out of the danger zone, slipping away so stealthily that the defenders still did not suspect the trap. It was too far to shout a warning, and in any case, such a move might precipitate the pitched battle which they were so anxious to avoid.

What might follow the diversion of the stampede, if the herd could be turned, could be equally vital. Both sides would be furious, the sheepmen as they understood the treachery of the murderous trick which had been aimed at them, the cowboys at its failure. To get between and try to deal with them at so excitable a moment would be at least as risky as trying to turn the rush, but again there would be no alternative.

'Once we get the cattle turned, you try and talk to your people,' he suggested. 'Calm them down if you can. I'll try and do the same with the cowboys.'

Sue nodded her understanding, but her eyes were anxious.

'If they don't shoot you on sight, they'll be ready to lynch you,' she pointed out.

'They'll have a job on their hands,' Nels promised laconically, and Sue reflected that, in some respects at least, this younger

Ondane was a lot like his uncle Bart. She managed a smile.

'Nels,' she said, 'I'm sure that if anybody can do it, you will!'

'Thanks,' he responded, and swallowed, finding his throat suddenly choked. 'All right,' he added, almost with relief. 'Here they come.'

Both were as well satisfied that there was no time wait, in which to think or count the odds. By now the herd, fairly compact to begin with, had been set in motion and, pressed hard from behind, they were quickening their pace to a fast walk. The riders remained silent, but flicking rope ends stirred the cattle to a trot. All at once, as the hitherto voiceless cowboys broke into a wild yelling, the herd swung into a mad run, heading precisely as had been planned.

The defenders could hear now, but could not see. By the time they understood, the trap would have been sprung. The vanguard of the stampede swept suddenly around a shoulder of hill, breaking past a line of big trees, and Nels kicked his horse in to a run, waving his coat and yelling like a madman. He was aware that Sue was right alongside, her shrill yipping beating at the oncoming tide of red.

It was a ticklish spot, even without the anger of the riders who pressed the cattle to greater efforts. To ride straight into the point of a madly running bunch and attempt to turn them was flirting with suicide. Should a horse stumble, it would be instantly overwhelmed, and its rider pinned under the avalanche of driving hoofs. Even if a horse kept its feet, once it was engulfed in the stampede, there would be plenty of risk.

Still, it was not all one-sided. The sudden appearance of riders in front, waving and shouting, coupled with the skill of trained cow ponies, worked as they had hoped. The leaders snorted, then swerved plunging at a new angle which would send them on a course safely to one side of the sheepmen. After that they could run as they pleased, spreading out and stopping, once their fright was over.

With the swinging of the leaders, the rest of the herd followed as a matter of course. Within a minute, most of them were heading away, and that peril had been averted. Sue fought her horse loose from among the herd, Nels pushing in to help her. But now the riders who had been pressing the herd came hard at their heels. They were joined by the others, who, having gotten back to their horses and finding themselves cheated, were fully as angry as Nels had foreseen.

There was one change in plan. Sue was leaving the sheepmen to their own devices, keeping her horse right alongside Nels'. As the two groups of cowboys converged on them, pulling up in a furious knot, Nels knew that it was probably only her presence which prevented them from shooting first and asking questions afterward.

A bear of a man, who filled his saddle to overflowing was clearly the leader. At the moment he seemed on the verge of apoplexy.

'What's the meaning of this?' he choked. Then his eyes narrowd with recognition. 'Why, you're an Ondane—and sidin' with those stinkin' sheepmen!'

It was a better opening than Nels had dared hope for, and he took quick advantage.

'Sure I'm an Ondane,' he agreed. 'As Bart's nephew, I'm heir to the Ox-Bow, and that makes me a cattleman.'

'A fine sort of cattleman, you! What do you think Bart would say to an Ondane sidin' with sheepmen?'

'Now I'm wondering about that,' Nels conceded, 'since Bart was a cattleman—and was murdered by those he thought were his friends!'

CHAPTER NINETEEN

Nels had counted on startling them, and it worked. Heads jerked at the word.

'Murder?' one man repeated. 'What you talkin' about? Bart went off to Highcard and died—but I never heard anything about murder!'

'Nobody heard about it, but that's what happened,' Nels assured them grimly. 'It's quite a story, and it concerns all of us, cattle and sheep ranchers alike. If you'll all hold off for a truce while I explain, I think you'll find it interesting.'

The beleaguered sheepmen, roused to their new peril, had moved out and swung about, making a cautious approach. Now, though keeping back, they were close enough to hear as he raised his voice. Suspecting a trick, they hesitated, and one of the cowboys growled a protest.

'You got any proof of what you're sayin'? Sounds to me like this was just a trick.'

'I can furnish all the proof that anybody wants, if you'll go and look at it,' Nels assured them. 'The rest of you, come close enough so you can hear this, too. It concerns everybody on both sides. I don't need to tell any of you about my Uncle Bart. You know what he was like, and I suspect that a lot of you hated him, cattlemen just as much as sheepmen. Which was fair enough, seeing how he hated everybody in turn.'

'That ain't very nice talk about a dead man, boy, even if he was as bad as you say. And him your uncle, and leavin' you his property.'

'All of you know that what I'm saying is true, and right now, the facts need to be aired,' Nels returned bluntly. 'I don't enjoy having to do it, for as you know, he left us the saloon. He did that, knowing how my Uncle August felt about liquor, because he figured that would cause trouble. Then, after arranging matters, he went off to Highcard and had word sent back that he was dead, so that his will would go into effect. Then he aimed to sit back and watch.'

There were perplexed scowls on more than one face. 'First you talk about murder; then you say he had some sort of a scheme, and went there to set back and watch!'

'I'm saying that was his plan. He aimed to work matters so that everybody in this valley would be at one another's throats—as you just were. When you had pretty well finished killing each other off, then he intended to show up again and grab control of just about everything.'

'Sounds like him, for a fact,' one man admitted.

'It was a workable scheme,' Nels agreed. 'Right then, you were starting to fight, just as he had planned. But the best laid plans can go wrong. When he got down near Highcard, before he ever reached the town, somebody shot him—in the back.'

'How do you know that?'

'Because his will provided that one of us, as his heirs, should go there and erect a marker over his grave. That marker, of course, would be proof enough for almost anybody, so that the fight would go on. I went there to carry out that provision and found him lying in a deserted cabin, a long way from the town, dying. He'd been shot weeks before, but had managed to survive that long. After I arrived, he lived just long enough to let me know that he'd had plenty of time to think and know that he'd made a mistake. It was too late to help him much. I buried him there. If anybody wants to have a look at the grave, or the body, it can be arranged.'

A thoughtful silence held while they digested that news. 'You knew about that when you got back up this way? Why didn't you say something then?'

'There were several reasons. It was too late to help him, and I figured I had a better chance to go on living if I didn't tip my hand, not until I found out just what was going on, and who was behind matters, now that he wasn't around any longer to work his plan. For it was clear that somebody was still trying to put it into effect.

'After I had buried him, I went on to Highcard, was told how he had died there, and was shown where he was supposed to be buried, just as he'd arranged for. That proved to me that something was rotten, and a lot closer than a country in Europe. So I didn't let on, but had the marker taken care of, then headed back—and found trouble already let loose through this valley.'

He had their complete attention now; there was an uneasy silence in which the resolving of some doubts created new ones.

'Today, I was accused of murdering Van Sickle, tied hand and foot, and thrown into a hole on the Ox-Bow. Then water was allowed to overflow from the irrigation ditch and spill down there, where I was scheduled to drown. Thanks to Sue here, I got out alive. And we get here to find you folks at each other's throats, just as everybody in the valley is supposed to be.'

He paused, looking at them wearily, and Sue caught his arm and steadied him as he seemed about to slump. He gave her a reassuring smile and straightened.

'Thanks, I'm all right. But you can all see that fighting each other isn't the answer. We're all neighbors, and should be able to get along. I'm not proud of what Uncle Bart schemed to do, but I'd like to see justice done, since I'm involved in this thing as deeply as anyone. What I'm afraid of is what may happen in town, unless we can get there fast enough to tell others the situation and put a stop to it, before those who killed Bart and took over his scheme get a war going.'

They viewed him with new respect, cattlemen and sheep barons looking askance at one another, somewhat shame-faced as understanding was forced on them.

'Me, I'd a lot rather be neighborly than

fight over nothing,' the big cowboy asserted frankly. 'I reckon it's only sensible to let you back what you've been telling us. If you can't, there'll be time enough for something else afterward.'

'Fair enough,' Nels agreed. 'So let's get moving. But keep in mind that when we get to town, we all work together, for the chances are pretty good that we'll run into a bunch of hot-heads, and maybe some hot lead.'

'He's telling the truth all the way,' Sue added quietly, 'if you're willing to accept my word.'

More than one of the cattlemen eyed her admiringly.

'Ma'am,' the big man returned gallantly, 'the way you helped turn that stampede here, nobody can accuse you of not havin' plenty of courage. And whatever some of us may think about sheep or sheepmen, why, nobody's ever accused the MacDonalds of toyin' with the truth.'

They set out for Mockery, their recent hostility shelved if not forgotten. Despite the exchange of a number of shots, no one had been injured, and that made it easier. Nels was both exhilarated and depressed, riding knee to knee with Sue. He would never have been able to manage without her; with her, he had the feeling that they could handle what might lie ahead.

As they came in sight of the town, dust was

rising from the hoofs of milling horses, which seemed everywhere. Mockery was crowded, and tension was as thick as the dust. More men had been arriving, from both factions. He had no doubt that every ranch was represented, and for once there was a curious likeness between sheepmen and cowboys. All were armed and ready for trouble.

Shooting had not commenced, but a quarrel was in progress. Apparently it centered around the new hardware store, which had been the big saloon only weeks before. Nels had a pretty good guess as to what the trouble might be.

There was no time here to talk, to try and explain that situation. That would take too long. Dismounting, he shoved through the crowd, Sue beside him. Men gave way reluctantly, but he was recognized, and today that made a difference. The big cowboy assisted on the other side.

Advice was shouted at him from both factions.

'You tell your uncle to use some sense and sell us those shells,' a cattleman advised. 'We ain't standin' for no more stalling!'

'If he gives all the means of killing to one side—why, we've still got enough ammunition to take plenty of others along with us when the shooting starts!' a sheepman warned in turn. 'And don't think we won't!'

Their coming had created a momentary

diversion; other action was being in abeyance until the crowd could learn what this nephew of old Bart might have to say. Nels shouldered through the open door. The room was packed now with supporters of both factions. August backed against the shelves behind the counter, was pale and determined, still unyielding.

'You'll have to kill me first, before you take a single shell!' he warned. 'With the situation as it is, and everybody spoiling for a fight, I won't sell to either side.'

'That's telling them, Uncle,' Nels called, and saw, not much to his surprise, that August was flanked, not alone by his wife, but by Mike and Janie Harris. Undoubtedly the presence of the women had delayed what must have otherwise exploded into violence.

'I've something for everyone to hear,' Nels added. 'Of equal interest to both groups of you. It's about how Bart Ondane was murdered—'

A six-gun made sudden thunder in the confines of the store, seeming to shake the very walls. Nels stared dazedly at the new hole in the wall, just beyond his head, even as shouts and struggle erupted. He had not seen Crockett, half-hidden behind the press of angry men, but desperation had driven the man to rashness. A smoking gun was in his hand now, though he had been unable, try as he would, to get off a second shot. He was struggling frantically in the grip of two men, one of whom was Larch Draine, pale hair showing crimson where Crockett had managed to slash defensively with the gun barrel.

CHAPTER TWENTY

Partial understanding came to Nels as he watched Crockett being subdued. Apparently he had edged in at a side door, fearful of what Nels might have to say, intent on stopping him at any cost. Larch, who Nels had supposed was half a day's ride away, had seen and interpreted such stalking and acted. Today he had repaid his debt.

Angry cries were going up as the crowd began partially to understand. An ominous refrain rose above the rest:

'String the shyster up!'

Crockett was being rushed toward the door and hustled along. Here was a ready vent for overcharged emotions. Whatever the animosity between groups, murder by treachery was outside the code.

Nels moved swiftly, getting in the way just at the open door. He checked the surge with some difficulty. 'Easy, now,' he cautioned. 'We don't want any lynch law here!'

'Maybe you don't,' was the good-humored

retort. 'But the rest of us do. He's got it coming to him. He tried to murder you, didn't he?'

'I guess he did, but since it was me that he was shooting at, seems like I should have some say about what to do with him,' Nels pointed out. 'I'll admit that it's a temptation to be rough with him. In fact, he's got it coming, but the law can do a better job. That's a better way to handle matters. Look how close we all came to being in a mess, with everybody ready to start shooting, some not even knowing half of what it was all about!'

The reminder had a sobering reflection, but he had to present a final argument to dissuade them.

'All right, I want him alive, not from any particular love for him or for the way he's been acting, but because I need him, and I have a notion that a lot of others in this valley will, too,' Nels insisted. 'He's been handling Uncle Bart's legal affairs, and he's probably acted as a lawyer for some of you. We know to start with that he lost his sense of honesty somewhere along the way, and that some of the matters he's been handling are in a bad mess. So some of us can be in a lot of trouble unless we have him to help straighten things out. Which I think he'll do, without requiring too much persuasion.'

Crockett was sweating, a slow trace of color seeping back to a face which had gone chalky with the imminence of the noose. He nodded eagerly.

'Sure, sure, I'll do anything I can—anything you say,' he promised. 'I'll fix everything up. It was all a mistake.'

'Maybe I'd better explain that,' Nels said, and went on to give an account of what had occurred, and how. There were still mutterings against Crockett, but most of the crowd were sobered at the reflection of how close they had come to disaster. Passions had been heated over a long period, but they were relieved at a chance to draw back. For the first time, there were friendly overtures between neighbors.

'I guess that's what we are, as Nels has pointed out—neighbors—and so we've got to live together,' a cattleman observed. 'Anyhow, there's plenty of room for all of us.'

'And there always has been, except that we've been too stubborn, too blind to admit it!' The speaker was an elderly man who had ridden up in a buggy, halting near the edge of the crowd. He sat quietly, with the air of a patriarch, but heads turned at his words, surprise and respect in most faces.

'MacDonald! Haven't seen you for a long time!'

MacDonald nodded, a wintry smile touching his face.

'No, I guess you haven't,' he conceded. 'And I haven't seen any of you lately. You see, I'm blind—but for the first time, I'm able to see clearly. Sometimes it takes that to enable a man to stop and think and gain a perspective. It's lucky for the rest of us that Bart Ondane had a nephew who could see farther than his nose.'

Sue had turned, startled, at the sight of old MacDonald. Now she hurried to him, and Nels was surprised that she greeted him as Grandfather, rather than Dad. Seeing the old man's blindness, Nels was beginning to understand.

'Here's Floyd, Grandfather,' she added. 'He's here, and he's been working all season as a herder, doing his best, and a fine job, too. He's made good, and he deserves a fresh chance.'

For just a moment MacDonald looked uncertain. Then he nodded, holding out a hand which the boy grasped eagerly.

'If Sue says so, then I must have been mistaken,' he admitted. 'I was as stubborn as anyone in this valley, as long as I thought I could see! You'll come home, boy?'

'I'll be glad to, Grandpa,' Clayton agreed.

Sue watched a moment longer with shining eyes, then swung back to Nels, and she came to stand beside him, his own vision was suddenly clear. Floyd was a cousin, not a lover; rejected for some past failure, he had returned secretly, able to do so because of his grandfather's blindness, realizing the old man's need of loyal help at such a time, willing to serve as a herder until he had proved himself.

The day had brought understanding and reconciliation in another quarter. Larch Draine, suddenly different, was talking to Janie Harris. But the warmth of Janie's welcome was not to be mistaken.

'You were wonderful, Larch,' she breathed. 'I always knew you had it in you, once you headed out on a straight trail!'

'Floyd and I talked things over, and then we headed for town, figuring this was where things were likely to happen,' he explained. 'I guess I've been just as blind as old MacDonald, but if you'll give me another chance—'

'You always insisted that I was your girl—and if you still feel the same way about it—'

Nels grinned. Then, with Sue beside him, he headed out of the crowd. Not that it made much difference. For the first time, everyone was greeting everyone else, relief and excitement tied in a surge of good fellowship. Nobody was paying any particular attention to him, except for Sue, and that was the way he liked it.

Photoset, printed and bound in Great Britain by
REDWOOD PRESS LIMITED, Melksham, Wiltshire